I0594124

First Printing, 2020

Cover by Bukovero
bukovero.com

ISKOMO

To Catherine.
Thank you for all your support, encouragement, and persistence.

ISKOMO

J. Bobeldyk

J. Bobeldyk

CONTENTS

CONTENTS

"Iskomo" Pete sat grudgingly at the bar turning the dirty, empty glass around with his fingers. There was a mixture of smudged fingerprints and small cuts that covered its surface, the result of the glass having been repaired three times too many. It was a typical Friday night at the Dive-In, a run-down bar which would never pass a health inspection. Instead, it served as a meeting place for the city's harder techheads and undesirables. Red neon lights hung behind the bar counter, providing a constant crimson glare that made up for the unstable, constant flickering fluro lights that took up the rest of the small area. In any of the dimly lit corners, some shady deal or exchange was taking place.

He toyed more with his glass of whiskey, wishing the bartender would have listened when he specified to leave the bottle. These drone bars never got anything right, yet he had considered it a personal win when he had been given actual whiskey. Something that tonight at least, was enough to convince him to stay. He glanced sideways to his right at the entrance, hoping to see some sign of his contact and sighed when he found it empty, yet again. To his left, the woman trying to get his attention was becoming harder to ignore.

"Fifty fundbytes will get you whatever you want honey," she purred, stroking Iskomo's leather jacket sleeve.

"For the last stinking time, not interested!" Iskomo sneered at her. He held up his left hand to show her a wedding ring. "Doesn't your programming recognise what the frag this means?" To his relief, the woman's expression turned blank as her holographic projection faded away only to reappear four seats further down from him at the bar, pestering another patron.

A scrawny man entered the bar, setting his guns down at the rack by the door. His balding head was covered with only a few tufts of frayed grey hair and his entire lower jaw was encased in metal. He noticed Iskomo and took the seat beside him.

"Sup, Iskomo, how's the wife?" the man asked as he sat. He placed a small datadisc on the bar between them and motioned at the drone bartender for two more drinks.

"I don't want to talk about her, and especially to you," Iskomo warned.

"Easy, easy," the man tapped the bar again as he glanced around. "I'm surprised you consider this dive stable. I didn't think your kind came to places like this."

"It's suited me over the years," Iskomo took the datadisc off the bar and concealed it in his jacket. "Now listen Marsack-o-shit, if this doesn't have the files on it..."

The man frowned. "It's Marcson, prick. If we're going to do business, you will need to be more respectful. And it's all there. Now maybe you can pay up so I can leave this shit hole." He waved off the drone setting down the two fresh whiskeys, "No offence."

Iskomo turned towards Marcson and reached into his left pocket and pulled out his b-card, ready to transfer the money. He waited until Marcson's eyes were focused on the b-card before he squeezed the trigger of the pistol he held in his other hand. The bullet hit Marcson in the chest, knocking him off the stool onto the floor, gasping.

Instantly the flickering lights in the bar became a steady stream. The holographic girls working for customers vanished and large metal security walls came down, sealing off every door and possible exit. A few people stood shocked at the gunshot, yet still craned their necks to see who was hit. The bartender drones had all retreated to a small hatch in the roof.

"I know you think you are hard," Iskomo said to Marcson as he knelt down above him. "Thinking this piece of metal is going to protect you from any major damage," Iskomo flicked the metal jaw with his fingers, the twang echoing around the silent room. "But I know what you did. And I tell you now, I don't give two frags if my hands end up as a bloody mush." Iskomo struck Marcson's metal jaw with his right fist, then followed it with his left. The clangs when his face was knocked to each side reverberated around the quiet room. "I'm going to show you, this techno shit isn't worth frag all." Iskomo continued to strike Marcson's jaw repeatedly. Each thud becoming sickeningly wetter as the metal buckled and Iskomo's fists tore more flesh open. "You chose the wrong wife," each word was followed by another hit to Marcson's jaw, now hanging loosely off his face as he gurgled. Iskomo stood himself back up and produced his pistol. His hands covered in blood and shaking violently, he took a deep breath and aimed at Marcson's head. The few patrons who were still silently watching did not move when the second gunshot rang out, the bullet ending Marcson's gurgling.

Iskomo looked around the bar, groaning as he put his aching hand into his pocket and pulled out his wallet. His hands trembling with agony, he opened it and held it up, showing it around in a wide circle for all the patrons and security cameras to see. "It's alright," Iskomo strained, a nervous chuckle following. "I'm with O.M.T." Iskomo noticed some of the patrons step back, slowly reaching into their own jackets or activating hidden software. "That," Iskomo pointed at Marcson's body on the floor, "was my only business here."

The next thirty seconds felt like an hour to Iskomo as he waited. A loud electronic series of beeps came from a speaker behind the bar, signalling a reset. The metal walls that covered the doors lifted and the music began to play again. On cue, the fluro lights began flickering once more and the holographic girls returned to visibility, apologising to their marks for their brief departure. Iskomo went back to his seat at the bar, downed the two drinks that had been ordered and walked out.

Outside he activated a voice link to the Society, an online network that had begun to incorporate all manner of communication. It served as a virtual network that users could plug into, either with direct hardware or by wireless augmentations. Using his own wireless system,

Iskomo sent an audio message through to the O.M.T. secured servers, without the hassle of needing a port or diving into the system online. It was originally one of the perks when he took the job, yet now the ability was commonplace. He usually preferred using his personal data assistant to send communications, but his intoxication made the digital letters dance in his vision.

"Iskomo, disc retrieved," he double tapped the side of his head and stumbled further into the night.

1

"Hello.

And welcome to the Oil, Medical and Technology Informant Hotline Channel.

Please wait as we verify your connection mode.

Thank you. You are connected virtually. Please wait as we check your informant credentials.

It appears you are not a member of the O.M.T. informant members club. If you would like to create an account now, please say so.

All information is treated with dignity and respect. We respect your choice, but for safety concerns, our servers have logged and time-stamped your Society access address.

Did you know as a member of the O.M.T. informant members club you can track your submission in real-time? Members can also set up personal alerts to their case to see hourly updates. You also will be eligible to receive the benefits of our rewards program, where every fifth successful submission case closure pays double the reward value. You can apply for this service at any time.

Please state the reason for your visit today."

Sarah shifted uncomfortably in her seat. It was for display purposes only, a bad habit of hers. While online in the Society it was acknowledged comfort was never a priority, but she had built up her online world through so much performance, it was hard sometimes for her to shake the act. While the female voice was performing its monologue she had taken the time to inspect her surroundings. The room she had ported into was cramped and small, the four walls around her completely white. There was no door, though she could not imagine why there would be need of one inside the virtual room. The single chair in the centre of the space where she sat made her feel like she was about to be part of a brutal interrogation. "Um, I think I was attacked earlier by an O.M.T. operative? I want to lodge a complaint?"

The female voice returned. "*If you have a complaint, please redirect yourself to our customer feedback server. Our operatives are fully trained professionals and do the dirty work so you don't have to. As company policy, only subscribers of the O.M.T. informant members club can request a consultation with an operative. Was there anything else today?*"

"Your operative went crazy on me!"

"*Please wait while we transfer you to the customer feedback server. We are experiencing delays of up to... three hours. To help our systems, please answer the questions provided to you by our survey.*"

"Subscribe me!" Sarah called out.

"*Welcome to the O.M.T. informant members club. Please answer verbally the following questions.*

Do you consent to your identity and Society address being stored with O.M.T.'s state of the art secure servers, for validation purposes?"

"Yes."

"*Do you consent to data collection from your online presence, informant tip history and locality being collected for the purposes of apprehending suspects?*"

"Yes."

"*Do you consent to O.M.T. collecting data from your history, including your offline whereabouts to help solve other case submissions?*"

"What? My offline whereabouts? You can do that?"

"*I'm sorry, please respond with a yes answer.*

Please respond with a yes answer.

Please respond..."

"Yes!"

"*Do you consent to paying a monthly fee of one hundred fundbytes for the cost of subscription? Please note no fees will be charged to you until your first submission pay-out.*"

"Do you mean you'll take the fee out of the reward money? That's...ugh, yes."

"Congratulations, Sarah, Blackwell. You are now a member of the O.M.T. informant members club. What is the reason for your visit today?"

"I told you. I was attacked by an O.M.T. operative today."

"If you have a complaint, please redirect yourself to our customer feedback server. Our operatives are fully trained professionals and do the dirty work so you don't have to. There are no submission cases being investigated for a Sarah Blackwell, so there is no reason an operative would have apprehended a Sarah Blackwell. Was there anything else today?"

Sarah screamed as she yanked the network plug from the back of her head, cutting her connection to the Society. Her apartment flooded her vision, she was still in her chair close to the network port in her bedroom. Sounds of the city outside crept in as her other senses also returned to normal, the smell of smoke coming from her kitchen.

Sarah slouched in her chair, taking it all in. She then snapped upright and ran to the kitchen, grabbing the pot that sat on the hotplate that was ablaze and threw it into her sink. She cursed at herself for being so absent-minded, aware though that she couldn't blame the lack of focus entirely upon herself. She activated the cooling system of the sink and watched with a fascinated curiosity as the metal sizzled and steam rose. Her apartment door opened and her roommate Cho entered holding a large tray of foodstuffs.

"What happened?" Cho nearly dropped the tray and rushed over to the sink.

"I was going to get all your stupid cooking things ready and hot, and, I got distracted," Sarah explained.

"It's not stupid," Cho laughed. "Science says relying on those little pills for nutrition is hurting us more than helping. This is the way nature intended." She motioned towards the groceries. "Are you alright though? Did you get hurt at all?"

"No. I'm just not used to all this mechanical cooking. Heat this, cut that. You can see how it died out. How did you even find this stuff?"

"The group that runs the plan, they gave me an infoslate that showed all the closest places that still stock this stuff. It's crazy Sarah, you actually have to go down and collect it yourself. It's retro."

"I don't know why you keep buying into these fads."

"I told you, it's health science," Cho gently brushed Sarah away from the sink. "This was the way it was. You'd prepare your food, cook it and then eat it. It's not just a novelty." She picked up the metal pot and looked at it. "They also said no refunds for damages, just saying. I wonder if this is still ok. You really should have waited for me."

"Yeah, sorry. It's just, my head is all over the place. I got attacked today." Sarah confided.

"It's not like you to be so out of it, what happened? Didn't your persec handle it?" Cho gave Sarah a sideways glance.

"My personal security system? It couldn't, it was weird."

"What?"

"It was this O.M.T. guy, he was cute too." Sarah began, she glared at Cho when she giggled to show this was serious. "We were just talking and then his attitude just changed, like that," Sarah snapped her fingers. "His whole demeanour changed and it scared me. I tried to back out and then he started chasing me. My persec didn't activate once and," Sarah cut herself off as she began to cry.

"That's mental," Cho moved towards her and hugged her. "You need to contact your persec manufacturer and lodge a complaint. It failing to go off is a serious error. What did he do to you?"

"Nothing, I got away. I just, he knew my name."

"Sarah," Cho pulled back and had a disapproving look on her face. "You didn't?"

"He knew my name, I didn't tell him."

"Alright, cause' you know the dangers of first name reveals? Did you forget about Monty?"

"Of course I haven't," Sarah reacted sharply. "I thought I must have met him before or something. Then he grabbed my arm and was reaching for his gun, and his face was just, I know he wanted to kill me."

"You need to report this to someone. Get in touch with your persec now. And I'd be contacting O.M.T. too," Cho turned back to her groceries.

"I tried already. I was so scared I came straight back here and tried to distract myself with your whole food stuff. Then I decided to try contact O.M.T. themselves and, I don't know. Nothing's worked. Their system won't acknowledge an operative's wrongdoing."

"Alright, well, firstly, let's calm down and we'll figure this out. If O.M.T. aren't listening I know a few media executives who would love a story like this. Why don't you relax, get some air or do something online, and I'll get some of this organised so we can try it out. Apparently it tastes quite different to the capsules. Then we can check in with some news bloggers."

Sarah weakly shrugged and nodded, returning to her room and sat back in her seat by the access port. She gave herself a few moments of sitting there quietly before locating her Society access leads and plugging the cable into the port at the back of her skull.

Online she became immersed in a haze of neon banners surrounding her. She grumbled to herself, realising her anti-ad subscription must have expired and opened a drop-down menu beside herself in the virtual world. She opened up her tasks tab and created a new entry, reminding herself to take care of that later. She backed out through the menus and opened her bookmarks. Sarah selected her webcast site and paced impatiently as the space around her morphed and rendered into a small recording studio she had designed.

It appeared like her own bedroom, except cleaner with better furnishings. She slumped herself onto the king size bed and faced a floating blank window which she used as the camera to record her casts. She always did her shows facing the camera directly, lying on her stomach on her bed. This was reported to build a sense of intimacy with the audience, and when everyone was competing for an audience, any advantage was huge.

She activated the recording mode of the screen and saw her projected online presence in the reflection. It was much like her, apart from the longer hair and unblemished skin. She could have spent a year fussing over details like which nose to use and the size of her eyes, but that would have been time wasted instead of pumping out content. She prepared herself as the timer on the screen counted down the seconds to when the stream would begin.

"Hi everyone, it's your gurl, TG Boston, checking in." Sarah made a peace sign with her digital fingers, also making sure she propped herself higher to expose more cleavage. Behind the projected screen she could see her donation counter ticking as it collected the incoming fundbytes. "Just a quick one today for all my wonderful followers. I think we'll take a look at some of the questions you have sent in."

She waved her hand and a hovering window appeared beside her in the recording that displayed the text to each question as she read them aloud. "First question, from R4nchm4n, how old am I? Well R4nch I'm sorry but I'd like to keep a few secrets, you naughty boy," Sarah gave the camera a suggestive wink and swiped to the next question. "Next one is from _23_Ego_23_, oh wow is that a legacy username? Anyways they ask; do I do private 1v1 chats? That's sweet, but to be honest if I did start a service like that it would be utterly unfair. There's so many of you and only one of me. I wouldn't have the time to have one on one conversations with each of you," Sarah bit her lip slowly as she finished talking, staring directly into the recording. In her wider vision, slightly out of focus she noticed the donation counter continued to climb. She focused back at the camera screen, letting her lip release from her bite. The donation counter appeared to increase pace.

"SilverBridgeDooDoo846," she giggled as she read the name, "asks what's my favourite colour." Sarah gave the camera a warm smile. "Oh that's sweet. You're a big softy one. My favourite colour is bright purple. Not neon or glow, just bright purple."

Sarah swiped her hand and began the next question. "Wow, only a few thousand to go. Sorry my fans but I did want to keep this one short today. I'm a busy girl. Leugenaar asks if I've ever considered becoming a real actress. That's what I'm doing now silly! Who wants to watch me pretend to be someone else when I can just interact directly with you guys here? Alright next question. TGBostonFan878 asks when my next giveaway is? Well stayed tuned cause' over the next couple of days I might have something for you."

"Well that's it for me today. I know, I know and I'm sorry it was so short." Sarah propped herself up more "As always, send me your comments and suggestions for my outfit for this Friday, voting closes Thursday at midnight Greenwich time. Links to vote are attached to the video source. Mwah!" Sarah ended the feed to the recorder and sat herself back up on the virtual bed. She checked her donation counter and sighed when it was only just over three thousand fundbytes. She accepted it was the drawback of doing such a short stream and closed down the studio, reloading the wider network of the Society.

She checked her incoming messages and discarded most of the fan mail. She would have a code bot autocheck and respond to that later. Her priority messages had one from Cho, empty except for the subject line; food is ready. Sarah logged off the Society and removed the cable from the back of her skull.

This time the aromas of unknown flavours filled her senses as they returned, something Sarah found much more appealing than smoke. "Wow, is that what food is meant to smell like?" Sarah called out as she felt her muscles returning. She stood up from her chair and walked out of her room to the dining area, tripping over Cho's body as it lay on the floor.

2

"Iskomo" Pete stumbled down the hallway towards the O.M.T. personnel area, the hangover in his head a constant throb now that his hands no longer hurt. He was aware he still stunk of the whiskey from the night before by the looks his colleagues gave him as he passed. Each one's face turning into a grimace that Iskomo himself found personally hilarious to mimic as he continued on. They were all younger than him, which to him meant they were all useless. Iskomo saw one of the few other agents he could tolerate, Neals, coming the opposite way towards him. Iskomo took the opportunity to lean against the white wall of the hallway, waving Neals to hurry up and come over to him.

"You look like shit," Neals announced when he got closer. "You need to snap out of this man."

"Well," Iskomo let out a heavy burp, forcing the bile that wanted to follow it back down into his stomach. "Got called in on my arrdeeoh, not my fault."

"Doesn't matter, everyone was meant to be in today, upgrading to the new patch. Where were you?"

"At the docs," Iskomo raised his right hand and showed it to Neals. "Needed some repair work."

"You punching walls again?"

"No," Iskomo chuckled to himself, drawing a concerned look from Neals.

"Did you finally upgrade to an aug?" Neals studied the hand.

"What? No! Shit in my head is bad enough, I'll be damned if I let them touch my hands. Keep it organic, feel that shit." Iskomo stumbled and slid against the wall.

"You're leaving a stain on the walls!" Neals gave Iskomo's shoulder a small backhanded slap. "You should have cleaned yourself up before coming in," he waved his other hand in front of his face, trying to escape Iskomo's odour.

"No time, haven't been home yet." Iskomo felt like he could sleep upright on that wall, if only his head would cease pounding.

"Well you're here now, head down and get patched."

"Frag that, I don't need it. I'll zero myself before I turn into one of them. Forget the patch, it's not why I'm here. I got a call from McCavern to head straight to his office." Iskomo tried pushing himself completely upright again.

"You need the patch Iskomo. I get your hang ups, but it has to happen. So, what did they call you in for?" Neals whispered.

"I have a suspicion, but don't worry about it." Iskomo saw Neals wanted a better explanation. "Scrapped Marcs last night."

"Ah, hence the hands. Kind of knew this was coming," Neals nodded. "Still, that doesn't explain-"

"I flashed the logo after."

"Shit man," Neals friendly smile was lost. "You can't be doing that; you know how stringy this mob is about P.R."

"They won't get rid of me. I'm untouchable," Iskomo grumbled. "All my assignments get resolved." Iskomo painfully winked at Neals and tapped his own forehead four times. "I got the knack."

"Yeah? I've heard that before, from a lot of people." Neals poked his finger into Iskomo's chest. "And they at least looked after their appearance. Maybe now you can get back on track yeah? Forget about all that shit with your wife and move on."

"Frag off Neals," Iskomo snapped back. "Let me self-destruct the way I want to. I got a meeting to be at." Iskomo lurched himself off the wall. He hesitated and gave Neals an apologising nod and pat on the shoulder. "I'll be fine. I always am."

"Who are you seeing again?" Neals asked before Iskomo got too far.

"McCavern."

"His office is the other way."

Iskomo let out a loud frustrated grunt and turned back around. A few agents walking down the hallway went wide of him as he marched back past Neals. "Thank you," he grumbled.

Neals nodded and then had his attention fall onto another agent passing by. Neals waved at the other and went running towards them. Iskomo didn't bother to check who Neals was meeting and continued down the hallway. The bright white lights were becoming less pain inducing, something he hoped signalled his hangover was finally subsiding. He eventually located the briefing room and saw McCavern sitting inside, typing away at the buttons that illuminated on his work desk. McCavern was similar to most Allocators; pale white from daily screen burn with half his face replaced by augmentations. His left eye had been replaced with a red lens that moved a floating holoscreen wherever he turned his head. Above it, the side of his skull was a layer of intricate metal and microchips with four Society connection ports running down where his ear once was. Why anyone would need four separate jacks into the Society was something Iskomo couldn't really make sense of, but McCavern had once assured him it was necessary. Assumedly it came with a much larger pay check.

The door unlocked and opened as Iskomo came closer, controlled by McCavern who motioned for Iskomo to take a seat. McCavern's human eye darted to Iskomo and back to his holoscreen repeatedly.

"How's the head?" McCavern asked blandly while he typed something into his desk's inbuilt lightboard. His hands stopped briefly and his one natural eye rested on Iskomo.

"How's yours?" Iskomo shifted in his seat.

"You wouldn't understand," McCavern's red eye also turned on Iskomo. Its brightness hitting Iskomo's vision like a laser.

"Can we just get this done?" Iskomo asked. "I had a busy day of nothing planned."

"Not anymore."

"What's the fine then?" Iskomo grunted, pulling out his b-card. "But the bastard had it coming, that's all I want to say."

"I'm aware of the situation," said McCavern.

"Neals?"

"Neals. Also you shouldn't drink too much of the real stuff," McCavern warned him. "Synthetic is ok, but actual whiskey? You got O.M.T. prime gear in your head and alcohol will just fry it." McCavern turned his head back to face the blank wall where his red eye projected his holoscreen onto it. "But that's not what's happening. You think up top cares about a little unofficial murder?" McCavern scoffed, his laugh ending in a mechanical squeal. "Course' not. But with the Quarterly coming up, bad press needs to be checked. We already know that Technix Colonies is digging for some story to hold over us." He typed something into his desk and a picture of a woman lying on a bed filled the wall.

"Who's the skinny?" Iskomo took a snapshot using his head's program, linking it to his pda.

"Skin cammer, goes by the username TG Boston. Real name, Sarah Blackwell. Yesterday she logs into the informant line and subscribes, requests a ticket and all that stuff. Her tip is she was attacked by one of our agents," McCavern softly chuckled again.

"Well that's clearly-"

"I'm not finished," McCavern stopped Iskomo. "She logs and live streams a quick skin show, gets all her fans drooling then relogs. Not five minutes later, before even her lobby has had a chance to clear out she jumps back on, shouting and carrying on about how she's been attacked twice by O.M.T. and how we're out to zero her. As you can imagine, she gets her fanbase all worked up and demanding action, petitions and all that useless shit."

The projected picture changed to a screenshot of the second video. The girl was back, looking terrified, and beside her a stream of comments from her audience had a theme of support.

"We shut down her channel. But you know this goes, the damage is already done. We can't let this go viral further and have it scooped up by Technix."

"Look at that comment count. Might be too late," Iskomo observed.

"We got a blanket out in time over the accounts. It won't hold though, you know how some of these kids are."

"Well it can't be a silence job, that'll just increase the theories." Iskomo pondered.

"Bullseye. Get to her, make a show of good faith, play at investigation and calm her down. Get her to recant everything publicly."

"It's a fan," Iskomo sighed and leaned back in the chair. "It's obvious, it's always the fans, stalkers the lot of them. Just have the bigwigs send out a press statement." Iskomo shrugged and looked at the door.

"It's been developed and they want this done." McCavern stated.

"Get Neals then, or anybody. You really called me in on my R.D.O. for this? Bullshit, McCavern."

"They wanted someone capable and more importantly, subtle." Mc-Cavern typed into his desk some more, and security camera feed began to play on the screen of Iskomo and Neals talking, finishing with Iskomo tapping his head and making the knack comment.

Iskomo stood up and kicked the chair away from him, cursing loudly. McCavern sat silently watching him and waiting. Iskomo's head swam from his sudden outburst and he balanced himself with one hand on the desk. "I had plans today!" He took a deep breath. "Full recant and I get triple rate," he told McCavern as he collected himself.

"Agreed," McCavern showed no sign of emotion and reduced the wall projection back to a floating screen. "You should have asked for more, the higher ups really want this dealt with." He made a waving motion with his hand and Iskomo's pda alerted him it had finished downloading the case files.

"I'm not coming in tomorrow," Iskomo scowled. He walked to the door and stopped, looking over his shoulder at McCavern. "Give Marth my regards."

McCavern nodded slightly and continued his focus on his work terminal. Iskomo exited the room and inspected his pda, scrolling through the files and checking all the usual information was there. He waved

Neals off as he passed him again, making his way to the building's entrance and stepped into the busy sidewalk of the street.

"Alright Miss Blackwell, let's go have a chat," he muttered to himself as he waved down a rideshare vehicle.

3

Iskomo's ride pulled up at the front of the apartment building where Sarah Blackwell was listed to reside. Outside the front entrance, a large black Titan Security van sat parked with a bunch of black armoured officers, puffing away on vapour cigarettes. They all turned and watched Iskomo as he approached the building. Iskomo dug into his jacket to locate his O.M.T. card when one of the security officers raised the reflective shield of his helmet.

"Iskomo, didn't realise this was O.M.T. business," the officer greeted him.

"Dagesh, is this where you spend your time now?" Iskomo reached out a hand to shake Dagesh's. "This your building?"

"It pays better, you should make the switch too." Dagesh looked up at the building, it was covered in neon advertisements that stretched up its entire body. "Yes, this is one of them. Titan holds the contract for a couple in this area. So, I guess you're here for the same reason as us?"

"What's happened?"

"Is this O.M.T. official?" Dagesh took another long drag on his vapour.

"I'm not going to close you out," Iskomo scoffed. "I couldn't give two shits about jurisdiction, I'm here to find Sarah Blackwell. Stop with the games and I won't get in the way."

"Alright Iskomo," Dagesh sighed, his face untensing. "Weren't sure if you were coming in with that big dick energy. Had a shootout two days ago in a building just down from here, that fragging Neals pulled O.M.T. backing and locked us out from it."

"So, what happened?" Iskomo asked again.

"Just some techheads who got too buzzed."

"The usual stuff. But I meant here." Iskomo pointed at the building.

"Alright so," Dagesh took a deep breath. "Techhead gets into the apartment of that Sarah chick and kills her friend." Dagesh tapped his black armoured arm panel and read out the data it displayed. "Stephanie Cho, online skin model. Takes a blunt object and repeatedly battered her face with it. Destroyed everything, organic, tech, the lot. Blackwell comes out and finds her, and the techhead tries to have a go at her."

"This was last night?" Iskomo noted what Dagesh was saying into his pda.

"She manages to lock herself in her room and puts the call out to the building management."

"She still alive?"

"Oh yeah, turns out she's a skin model as well. The bedroom door had all sorts of security on it."

"Just not the front door?" Iskomo mumbled.

"Blackwell thinks Cho may have left it open. Anyway, management log it to us and we arrive to find him still in the apartment, carving shit into the wall. He did come quietly. Was disappointing I'll admit."

"I don't have any of this information," Iskomo refreshed his pda and checked for updates.

"Closed system, sorry Iskomo, but O.M.T. doesn't always know everything. Anyway, he's set for delivery."

"You have him still?" Iskomo's head lifted to stare at Dagesh directly.

"In the van," Dagesh pointed to it over his shoulder. "You want to question him? We're not getting anything here."

Iskomo put his pda down and stared at the van, scratching the stubble on his chin. "When did you apprehend him?"

"Early hours this morning, about four a.m.."

"You haven't taken him back to your holdings?" Iskomo asked. "Fair warning, I'm still a bit hungover, yeah? I'm just a bit confused by this timeline."

"We had orders to hold him here, for you I'm guessing now," Dagesh said.

"Well," Iskomo tried to think. "Get him out of here for now. My case is to talk to Blackwell directly, totally different matter."

Dagesh laughed. "Good luck Iskomo, she was very vocal about O.M.T. when we tried to collect a statement." Dagesh lowered his visor and turned back around to his colleagues. He made a circle motion with his hand pointed upwards and the officers stood up from where they rested against the van and began moving.

Iskomo entered the building and took the exterior elevator up. With its glass windows he could see the surrounding parts of the city. He slowly backed away from the glass as it rose higher. More came into view. Other residential blocks that glittered with neon promises of delivering instant gratification were becoming dulled by the brightness of the day. In the distance to his right, the headquarters of O.M.T. stood, towering above the green parklands that surrounded it and the monorail lines that fed into its belly. On Iskomo's left, the fortress-like tower of Technix Colonies lay in opposing threat, facing off against their competition.

The elevator chimed and offered Iskomo an experience survey which he rejected, exiting before its next offer. The first thing he noticed was the hallway floor had carpets, something that had seen less use after so many mechanical feet would snag themselves on the fibres. He walked along the hallway, eyes drawn to the blue carpet below him, trying to experience the sensation as best he could through his shoes. A door slammed shut down the hallway ahead of him bringing his focus back to his case.

He found the listing of Blackwell and knocked on the door, placing his O.M.T. card against the registry to identify himself. "Sarah Blackwell?" Iskomo attempted his best friendliest voice. "I'm from O.M.T." There was no answer from inside. Iskomo could hear movement of something scrambling around.

"Blackwell?" he tried calling out again. "Acknowledge or I will be forced to breach the door."

"Leave me alone," Sarah's voice screamed back.

"Stand back from the door, I'm breaching," Iskomo called out, unholstering his pistol.

"Wait," the panicked reply came. "I'll open it."

The door to the apartment slid open and Iskomo came face to face with Sarah Blackwell. She didn't resemble her file image at all, her hair was wildly frazzled and her eyes and nose were red and swollen. Her face was streaked with smudged make-up. Her fear swapped to confusion as she took in Iskomo's own appearance, unshaven, unclean and the smell of alcohol that radiated from him. Her eyes dropped down to see the gun in his hand and she screamed, trying to slam the door shut again.

"Wait," Iskomo yelled and lunged forward, catching both his foot and arm in the door.

Sarah fell backwards onto the floor. She quieted down and lay still on the floor. "You know what? If you're going to frag me then just do it. I can't anymore."

Iskomo entered the apartment and shut the door behind him, holstering his pistol. "I'm not going to frag you," he scolded her. "My name is Isk... Peter. I was sent to review your tip line case."

Sarah continued to lay unmoving on the floor. Iskomo scanned the apartment's layout, recording it. It was the one of the higher tier layouts. The designs reserved for those with the larger sources of incoming fund-bytes More than what some skin model should be drawing. Either this Sarah Blackwell was the rare kind who found real virtual success, or a spoiled brat of some loaded parents who got her kicks teasing flesh. Deep gouges were cut into the designer wall. Iskomo made a note of the design, two oval circles reaching outward, separated by a long vertical line between them. He turned back to Sarah, irritated by her display of patheticness.

"Get up," Iskomo angrily ordered her. He reached down and took hold of one Sarah's arms to hoist her back up. When his hand gripped her skin a sharp electric shock plunged into Iskomo's arm and he recoiled, cursing in pain. "Turn off your fragging persec kid, I'm trying to help." He stomped his foot on the ground repeatedly, hoping it would dull the pain running up his arm. "Fragging hell that shorted me out!" he tried accessing his internal connection to the Society, resulting in errors.

Sarah sat herself up slightly, studying Iskomo. "I was under the impression persec's didn't work against O.M.T.?"

"What?" Iskomo continued to stamp his foot and shake out his arm. "Well obviously they do." He continued to mutter about the pain. "Deactivate that shit and get up."

Sarah's eyes dropped to the floor in thought. "I don't believe you're O.M.T. You certainly don't look it. And yesterday my persec didn't even affect an agent. So no, I don't think I will."

Iskomo tried to show her his O.M.T. card. "I'm official. I was sent to review your case. You publicly accused O.M.T. of some untrue things last night. My job is to discover why."

Sarah stood herself up. "Untrue?" Her voice raised. "Untrue? An O.M.T. agent did attack me yesterday. Then my roommate was murdered and I spend all night trapped in my room. Yeah. I went online and told everyone. Big surprise, now you bunch are finally off your arses and doing something."

"This guy last night? Same person?"

"No. Completely different. Doesn't that prove I've been targeted?"

"Your roommate's attack is most likely unrelated," Iskomo coldly spoke from experience. "I'm here because you claim an agent attacked you without objective justification."

"One did."

"I believe you saying that someone attacked you, but it wouldn't have been an O.M.T. You're a skin model correct? Most cases like this it's a fan, probably dressed up as an O.M.T. to get close to you."

"Frag you," Sarah snapped back. "This guy grabbed me, held onto me and my persec didn't go off like it did to you just now."

"That's not my thing. You'd need to reach out to your persec supplier for that." Iskomo started looking around the apartment, intrigued by the pans and whole foods that lay on the benches.

"Ok what?" Sarah scoffed.

Iskomo drew his attention back to Sarah. "Hmm?"

"You clearly have more to say on that subject."

"Uh."

"Go on, say it." Sarah crossed her arms.

"Alright," Iskomo shrugged and stared her directly in the eyes. "You sure you didn't deactivate it yourself? Fan comes along, they're a big one too, obsessed, so they know everything to get your attention. You're thinking they're just a nice and fun, appealing person. You deactivate your persec cause' you're thinking this is going to turn to physical fun real soon."

"I didn't deactivate my fragging persec."

"Hey, I'm just speaking from past experience with cases like this alright?" Iskomo explained. He took out his pda and cleared his throat. "Let's get this over with. Any details you missed in your first log? Give me the what, where and who. I'll find this guy and prove he's just another rogue fan."

"What about the guy last night? My friend?"

"I'll determine whether it's worth looking into."

"Are you fragging serious? Are you really fragging being serious right now? Are you a fan of mine, I mean, do you know who I am?" Sarah asked.

Iskomo shrugged, still awaiting to input data into his pda, "No idea. Just help mc help you, agreed?"

"What the frag?" Sarah clenched her fists. "Is this how you handle all your reports?"

"Usually we don't have to meet with an informant," Iskomo looked up. "They tend to give us all the information we need at the start of a case. When did this attack occur?"

Sarah pointed at the floor. "This one? Or the O.M.T. one?"

"The one with your fan," Iskomo's pda emitted an alert that he had a new message from Dagesh. "Why is he messaging me? Listen, could you just give me a minute before we continue?" Iskomo didn't wait for Sarah's answer and opened the message on his pda's display screen.

Iskomo, some interesting info being dumped from the tech head. You might want to drop by and ask some questions yourself. We'll put him on ice til' you get down here.

Iskomo quickly tapped a reply to the message. *Like what?*

The reply from Dagesh was instant. *Divers revealed the tech head was there for Blackwell. Thinks he succeeded too.*

Iskomo let out a groan as he read it.

"What's going on?" Sarah asked, backing away from Iskomo.

Iskomo lifted his head to face her. "Just, complications." He swiped his pda back to the case files for Sarah and looked again into the residential data. "Cho was your roommate you said?"

"Yes." Sarah wiped a tear away from her eye. Her face was a mixture of rage and grief. "I didn't think I'd still be able to cry after the amount I did last night." She weakly let out a soft chuckle.

"The listing for this apartment only has your name," Iskomo said as he read the files. "Doesn't mention..."

"Stephanie."

"Sorry. Stephanie Cho isn't listed anywhere in the occupancy."

"What does that have to do with anything?" Sarah asked.

"The Titan boys say they've pulled data to suggest your roommate's murderer targeted your apartment believing you were the sole occupant."

"So he was after me?" Sarah announced with grim realisation.

"Yeah, it's possible. I will need to go check for myself."

"So I was right!" Sarah yelled at Iskomo, pointing angrily at him.

"Shut up and listen," Iskomo warned her. "Could just as easily have been another fan. Has your Society port or address been compromised recently?"

"Everything I do is under an alias," Sarah sneered. "I'll be demanding an apology."

Iskomo grumbled but continued. "No chance someone has infiltrated your accounts and mailing lists?"

"My anti-ad subscription has seemed to have ended early," Sarah added.

Iskomo pondered it for a moment. "No, I don't think that's anything," Iskomo disregarded the detail. "Ok, where were we? Ah, nearly forgot. So under O.M.T. protocol it lists you as a subscribed member, yadda, yadda, yadda. Would you like to receive tracking and hourly updates?" Iskomo stared at Sarah, shaking his head.

"Yes," Sarah stated.

Iskomo cursed under his breath, fully intending Sarah to notice. "Ok fine. Just so you know all this will be resolved in an hour, so here's your only update. I'm going to investigate the man who attacked Cho last night and find what the deal is there. I'm positive it'll reveal some breach in your Society security and confirm this is just another fan attack. Then I'll be back for resolvement."

"Wait," Sarah stepped forward. "You're leaving?"

"Well, I'm on the clock here."

"Hey! What about my channel? You guys locked it down, when will that get lifted?" Sarah demanded.

"When I prove this is fan related, you'll need to provide an identifiable recant of your accusations against O.M.T. that you made last night. Then any locks can be removed. Please don't argue with me about that, not my department." Iskomo turned to leave.

"I'm very fragging unhappy with the service I'm receiving! One hundred percent bullshit!" Sarah yelled after him as he walked. Iskomo didn't turn around but continued to walk into the elevator, giving a backhanded wave to her. "You also stink like shit!" Sarah called out finally, before slamming her door again. She hit the panel beside her door, and the sound of locks being activated echoed through the hall.

4

Corporation buildings were all the same. From each hallway to door arch, buildings had become mass produced, turning each one into a clone of the other. The only noticeable difference being which brand or logo was emblazoned on its walls. Residential towers, business conglomerates, even the rare marketplaces with their promotions of nostalgic design. If you had seen one, you knew the basic layout of them all. Humans were still prone to change little things, which room was used for what purpose, but it was still mostly the same. Bars hadn't, which is why Iskomo frequented them after his shifts. Each bar was distinct from the previous. It was the last true form of social interaction left which had to still encourage its customers to leave, and actually get out and participate in. Online narcotic markets had attempted to gain a foothold in the Society, but it didn't account for how misery loves company. It was a group activity that couldn't be replicated online. Not yet.

Iskomo wandered into the Titan Security lobby and from sheer repetition found himself at the sign in terminal. Waving his O.M.T. badge under the scanning laser he yawned as it asked him the purpose of his visit. "Other," he mumbled as he tried closing his mouth. He rolled his hands in front of him, gesturing the terminal to hurry up.

The terminal began its second audio question, abruptly pausing when Iskomo interrupted. "Concise rubber station," Iskomo told the terminal, his foot now tapping as he waited.

"I'm sorry. I don't understand, transferring you to a representative now," the terminal dinged, Iskomo letting his head fall back in a small show of victory.

The terminal's screen was replaced with the image of a woman with long black hair, pulled tight into a ponytail behind her. She wore glasses and stared directly at Iskomo.

"How will I help you today?" she asked, her face showing no sign of emotion.

"Frag me, that's new," Iskomo paused and looked closer at the screen. "I didn't think you lot ever showed your faces."

"Titan Security is the leading security provider to over twelve districts…"

"Ah shit, another A.I." cursed Iskomo. "Alright, keywords. Iskomo, Pete, Dagesh, today's date."

"One request found. Welcome. Please follow the guided path on the floor." The avatar of the woman faded away and was replaced with the usual visitor terminal welcome screen. Iskomo shook his head at the attempt it made and looked to his feet.

Around his body, a small yellow circle had illuminated on the floor around him, with a directional arrow. As he stepped forward the circle moved with him, it's arrow sliding to continue to point in the direction it suggested. Iskomo groaned and followed it, passing down hallways and into an elevator. The lift automatically selected his floor and the arrow was replaced with a flat hand palm, flashing red. As the doors opened, the arrow revisualised again and Iskomo continued, coming to another small lobby where the circle disappeared.

One of the doors to Iskomo's left opened and Dagesh stepped out, waving at Iskomo. "Just got the alert. I'll take you down now, just need to take him off ice."

"Pig loops? You serious?" scoffed Iskomo. "That tech was old when it first came out."

Dagesh considered the question for a moment. "What? I think the administration still uses that for people without the latest ocular biometrics."

"Fix your systems," Iskomo grumbled.

"Fix yours, when was your last diagnostics?"

"This morning," Iskomo answered, rubbing his hands. "Mechanics did a check while they repatched my knuckles. Ah shit, Neals did mention something about a new patch."

"Right, well, probably that then. Follow me," Dagesh began walking down the hall, Iskomo following. "Titan wants to cooperate with O.M.T., which is amusing given the climate. Either way do you want to dive or dissemble or what? Honestly though, I'd recommend diving. The guy is scrambled."

"Live interrogation," Iskomo answered. "Do me a favour and make sure any inhibitor software he has is disabled."

Dagesh laughed. "We're not rookies Iskomo. This is it, we use this room for the lives, everything else is automated and come see me after for the recording. Anything else you need?"

"Nah, I'm good. Thanks."

"Do you consent to me witnessing the exchange from observation, and cloning the recording for future training purposes?" Dagesh asked.

Iskomo raised a hand to cover his face. "Fragging hell. Yes, whatever." He pushed the door open and went inside.

The room was bare apart from the chairs and table that grew out of the ground, unable to be moved. Dagesh's voice came over the intercom, the speaker inside a small grate on the roof. "Any preferences?"

"You got generic?"

"There are ten options for generic."

"Give me seven," Iskomo groaned, waiting as the holographic overlay loaded over the room. The room became a scene in grayscale, the walls shading themselves and the chairs and table textures changed with it. "Frag, no, just make it version one," Iskomo ordered. The colours came back into the room and the chairs took a shape of steel bars. The walls covered themselves with flaking concrete and a small fan hung from the ceiling, spinning slowly.

"Lose the fan, keep the rest," Iskomo said, shifting himself into the chair as the fan depixelated. "Bring him in."

A panel in the roof above the chair opposite Iskomo slid open and the torso was lowered from it. The legs and arms were removed, leaving a biomechanical frame held in place with clamps that lowered it into the chair. From the back of the neck, long cables ran back into the roof.

"Frag, you were almost pure mech," Iskomo observed.

"One second Iskomo, he's still sedated," Dagesh spoke over the intercom.

The body lurched and the head shook violently, rocking back and forth as it took in its surroundings. It settled and faced Iskomo, looking him up and down, sniffing the air in disgust.

Iskomo gave a small wave to properly grab attention. "I'm from O.M.T., here to ask you some questions."

"Are you my defence?" the man asked, still looking around the room.

"No, I'm from O.M.T., here to talk to you about the girl you murdered." Iskomo leaned forward. "Is he still sedated?"

"Dampeners were purged fully," the intercom buzzed.

"He still seems out of it," mumbled Iskomo.

"He was like that during our first analysis too, must have some wires crossed."

"Right," conceded Iskomo. "So," he announced, clapping his hands, "you got any gang affiliations? You look pretty geared up."

"Perks of the job," the man answered.

"What job is that?"

"Courier."

"Really? Fragging hell and they load you up with all that?"

"Why can I smell you?"

"Let's start with you. What's your handle?" Iskomo dismissed the question aimed at him.

"I can't remember," the man said, frowning.

"You can't access that? But you're aware of your occupation?"

"Yes, like I said, I'm a courier."

"Which organisation?"

"Uh," the man's head shook. "Are you my defence?"

Iskomo leaned back in his chair. "Dagesh?" he yelled at the intercom, "What the frag man? Purge him again."

"There's nothing left in his system to purge. I did warn you a dive would be easier," Dagesh responded.

"What do you remember?" Iskomo asked the man. "Tell me about the symbol you were carving into the wall when they arrested you."

"From when?"

"From last night. The murder? You attacked and killed Stephanie Cho last night."

"No I killed Sarah Blackwell."

"Stephanie Cho. Sarah Blackwell was trapped inside her room. Still very much alive."

The top left of the man's augmented head gave a quick spark and he jolted. "I killed Sarah Blackwell."

"What was that?" Iskomo asked the walls.

"He's uploading something." Dagesh called out.

"Your rooms aren't sealed?" Iskomo jumped up from his seat, checking the man's neck ports for any loose cables.

"They are, he's locked down. I don't understand how he's doing it." Dagesh sounded nervous.

"Get a copy of whatever he's transmitting, try work out where he's trying to send it." Iskomo ordered. "Hey, hey!" He snapped his fingers in the man's face. "Why did you want to kill Sarah Blackwell? Are you a fan of TG Boston?"

"Who is that?" the man's head bobbled, his eyes rolling back.

"Skin cam, admit it, you're a fan, wanted to taste the real thing," Iskomo flinched back as another spark burst from the man's temple.

"My name is Rory Alcanter. I work for Carolco Express. I murdered Stephanie Cho. This is my confession." the man, Rory, stared Iskomo in the eyes as he spoke with a strange calmness.

"Why? Actually, frag it, good enough." Iskomo pointed his finger up, spinning it clockwise.

The clamps holding Rory began to raise him back into the roof. He returned to scanning the room, eyes wide and scared. He settled on Iskomo before he was taken out of view. "Are you my defence?"

"That confession good enough for you?" Iskomo asked aloud.

"It'll work. Meet you outside."

Iskomo left the interrogation room and caught Dagesh leaving observation. "Scrambled alright."

Dagesh nodded. "Happy to call it. O.M.T. want hand over?"

"No, you guys take him. Leaving penalty to your discretion, I'll just update my end of things." Iskomo pulled out his pda and began entering data. "Got a witness anywhere close?"

"Yes," Dagesh looked around, "down here."

The two walked past the interrogation rooms towards a large steel security door at the end of the hallway. Dagesh pulled a cable from the wall panel beside it and plugged into the back of his neck. The panel turned green, Dagesh removing the cable as the door slid open. Inside two men in clear plastic bodysuits worked over a table of microchips and processors.

"Need a witness," Dagesh called out to them as they rose from the table.

The man on the left groaned and walked over to them, taking off his gloves. He reached into his pocket and pulled out a datacard, "Can I just scan? It's too much trouble taking all this off to port in."

Iskomo nodded. "Sure. Confession, if you're curious."

"Whatever," the man waved his card at Iskomo's pda, stared at it until it beeped a verification then returned back to the table.

Dagesh motioned for Iskomo to return the way they came. Iskomo checking the time on his pda, it had not been an hour yet, no update needed. "Did you get a copy of what Rory was trying to send?"

"Some of it, wasn't expecting it. It's all encrypted. Will need to get a bit jockey onto it."

"I'll take it as is, O.M.T. can decrypt it there." Iskomo stated, purposefully speeding up his pace.

"No," Dagesh said, causing Iskomo to stop and turn back to him.

"No? What happened to all that cooperation you were shovelling before?"

"The fact that this was even attempted, is a Titan Security matter. I can't let this get out yet. We will need to access the entire interview, find out why the dampeners..."

"Yeah alright," interrupted Iskomo as he began to walk again. "Just give me a copy as soon as it's decrypted. Give me the interrogation file at least?"

Dagesh stepped into the observation room and quickly came back out, catching up to Iskomo. "Should be receiving now."

Iskomo checked his pda, seeing the downloading bar fill completely. He brought up the video feed, scanning it forward until Rory's confession. "Trim and cut, create new file." Iskomo told his pda. "That's the juice of it there. Good seeing you Dagesh," Iskomo called as he left. "Remember, the transmission files!"

Iskomo made his way back to the lobby of the building and went for the doors. As he approached, a large holographic window blinked into existence in front of him, wishing him to return soon and offering him a customer survey. He tapped his head, closing the window from his view and remarked to others that were walking into the building, "now it works!" confusing them. "Pig loops!" he announced again, it echoing in the foyer as other people tried avoiding eye contact.

He exited the building and waited for a rideshare, going through a checklist on his pda. "Done, done, done," he mumbled as he checked each point off. He accessed his inbuilt Society uplink and compiled an audio. "McCavern, possible i.d. on the Blackwell case. Rory Alcanter. Priority." He sent the file to McCavern's O.M.T. address and sync'd his pda to his personal systems. Checking the time on his pda matched his internal clock he groaned, "Just under an hour, I hate always being right."

5

"You're back already?" Sarah scoffed at Iskomo as he stood in her doorway. "No way."

"O.M.T. prides itself on efficiency," Iskomo sarcastically replied, walking into the apartment.

"Well? What happened? Where did you go before? Do I get my channel back now?"

Iskomo pulled out a chair and sat at the clutter filled table. "I went over to Titan. Checked out that techhead that killed your friend last night."

"And?"

"And he confessed, when I'm finished, I can provide you a copy of his confession if you want. Some informants collect them, trophies or something."

"Why would I want that? And what, that's it?" Sarah began pacing back and forth in the living area of the apartment. "What about the O.M.T. who attacked me?"

"I got a suspicion it's the same techhead," Iskomo kicked out a seat in front of Sarah, motioning for her to take a seat.

"It wasn't the same man," Sarah insisted as she continued to pace, dodging the chair.

"I've got H.Q. checking some stuff now. It's a lot faster when we got a name rather than trying to filter the database for an image match."

Sarah stopped and took a deep breath. "You haven't listened to anything I've said. I was attacked. My friend was murdered! And not by the same fragging guy! We're not people to you, are we? We're just some numbers on a case file or some shit."

Iskomo shrugged. "Yeah."

"Asshole," Sarah raised her hand as she marched towards him.

"I wouldn't," Iskomo warned her. "Assaulting an O.M.T. agent during his investigation will void any informant reward."

"Frag the reward!" Sarah screamed at the top of her voice. "I just want to know why this is happening?"

"Sit." Iskomo pointed to the chair again. "I still need your public recant."

Sarah slumped down into the chair. "No."

"No?"

"You haven't resolved my case."

"Hey listen for one second," Iskomo growled, "You don't decide shit, I decide when a case is closed. Why don't you make like a good little informant and just wait for the resolution report."

Sarah took more deep breaths, calming herself down. "Why are you here then?"

Iskomo watched as Sarah rubbed her eyes dry, her black eyeliner smearing further across her face. "I wanted to be here when they returned an ID for your attacker," he found himself talking softer than usual. "Just..."

"Just proving you were right?" Sarah nodded her head in agreement. "Wow, you really are an asshole."

"Whatever," Iskomo scoffed. He received an alert on his pda informing him McCavern had responded. He attempted to access the file with his internal systems, resulting in error messages. "Fragging hell," he complained pulling out his pda. "Why is nothing compatible anymore?"

"What?" Sarah asked as she watched him.

"Nothing," Iskomo opened the same file on his pda, the audio playing instantly.

Suspect confirmed. Rory Alcanter. Security footage secured from LumoDigital. Rory Alcanter confirmed in proximity to Sarah Blackwell at current time minus seventeen hours.

Iskomo clapped, standing himself up. "What time yesterday were you attacked? About six p.m.?"

Sarah sat there watching him, speechless.

"So," Iskomo placed both hands on the table, staring at Sarah. "About that recant."

Sarah shook her head, "It wasn't him, it wasn't the same guy."

"They got vidfeed showing he was there. Listen, it happens. You met him once, talked, later he comes and tries to attack you again. You don't recognise him cause now, he's a monster. Brain does funny things to protect itself."

"Why won't you believe me?" Sarah begged.

"I need you to provide that recant." A door chime buzzed through the apartment, distracting Iskomo. "You expecting someone?"

"I don't know, no." Sarah slumped herself into a ball on the chair. "Stephanie... used to get deliveries all the time. It's probably something she ordered yesterday."

Iskomo walked over to the door, "I'll tell them to come back. That recant is priority." He pressed the controls and opened the door. As it slid open, Iskomo found himself staring at the bulky chest of a heavily augmented docker. Construction workers who utilised union resources to replace their limbs with heavy machinery. Iskomo's eyes raised up to the jawline of the docker, his chin was twice the size of Iskomo's and covered in thick black stubble. His eyes were hidden behind a set of welding safety googles. "The frag?" Iskomo blurted out as the docker swung low at Iskomo. His right arm replaced with a piston hammer that connected with Iskomo's chest and launched him backwards into the apartment. Iskomo hit the ground beside where Sarah sat. She launched herself upright, screaming and ran for her bedroom door. Iskomo regained his senses and fought through his blurry vision to see her door slamming shut. He rolled to his side, his chest full of hot pain and tried to push himself up.

"O.M.T.," Iskomo identified himself as the docker approached him. It raised its piston hammer again above where Iskomo still lay. "Frag," he muttered and rolled himself away, narrowly dodging the strike as it connected with the floor. The blunt edge of the hammer reverberated against the reinforced floors and shook the whole apartment. Iskomo rushed to his feet as the docker spun again to face him. "Attacking an O.M.T. agent during an investigation is a class 4 crime shithead," Iskomo wasn't sure if he was ordering or begging. He moved himself between an island bench in the kitchen as a barrier. He reached to his holster and pulled out his pistol. The docker closed the small gap between them and knocked the pistol out of his hands before he could fire it. The dockers other arm swung at Iskomo, a large clamp used for repositioning heavy trade pallets. Iskomo ducked below the arc of the swing, knowing if his head was caught in its vice grip there would be no reconstruction surgeon on earth who could repair the damage.

The docker moved himself between Iskomo and the pistol, coming around the side of the island bench. Iskomo backed himself against the benches that lined the kitchen walls, studying his opponent for an exploit. The clamp and piston hammer was oddly hydraulic, and his body betrayed the tell-tale lines and curves of ceramic sculpture. The goggles protected him from any cheap exploits that blinded others and his pistol would be useless against the body frame.

Iskomo ducked as the docker lurched forward again, driving his piston hammer into the cabinet that was behind Iskomo's head. It ripped its arm back, tearing the cabinet off the wall, the contents spilling onto the floor.

Trip ya bastard, Iskomo thought as he saw the organic fruits roll around them. The docker was fast with its strikes but slow moving, the weight of his frame and augmentations more suited to relocating cargo holds. He came at Iskomo again. Iskomo feigned towards the docker, who struck out again with the clamp at the chance. The dockers foot crushed an apple, and with the weight and momentum it sent him tumbling forward onto the ground. Iskomo jumped onto the dockers back and moved behind him. Iskomo reached down at the fruits and collected as many as he could in the panic. The docker was slowly up righting itself but now Iskomo was behind him. As he had hoped, Iskomo noticed the backs of the docker lacked armour and he had a clear line of sight to the hydraulic gears. In a desperate effort, Iskomo began trying to force the fruits into the systems of the docker. Apples and bananas burst and squished themselves between the gears. Their juices flowing down to the circuits hidden below.

Now free a hand, Iskomo tore at the dockers shirt, ripping it down and looking for more openings between the sculpted ceramic torso. He saw one running down the spine and ripped it away with his free hand. Inside more mechanisms twisted and turned. "Fragging hell," Iskomo swore at the sight. He planted more fruits inside the pistons, squeezing them hard into the frame. One gear twisted and caught his fingers, crushing them. "I just had those fragging repaired!" Iskomo cursed in agony, trying to free himself. He felt his fingers tear away as he pulled back, looking at the bloodied stumps in almost horror.

The mechanisms inside the docker seized with the blood that remained with the fruit juices. A piston emitted a loud grinding sound and a small burning spark flung itself at Iskomo. The docker slumped forward to the ground with a heavy thud and lay unmoving, small puffs of smoke coming from his back. Iskomo hobbled towards his gun across the room and snatched at it. He moved back towards the downed docker and placed the barrel of his pistol against the dockers head and unloaded the clip, screaming in pained anger as he did. Tossing aside the empty gun he fell back to the floor, yelling as loudly as he could muster, "Sarah! Get your ass out here!"

It felt like an eternity, but Sarah opened her bedroom door and brought her hands to her mouth at the scene. She avoided the docker, edging around the corpse while continuing to stare at his demolished skull. She saw Iskomo on the floor clutching his stump fingers, tears streaming from his eyes. "Holy shit," she kept repeating the phrase over and over.

"I shouldn't have done that," Iskomo winced. "Fragging."

Sarah lent down and tried to help Iskomo up. He convulsed and screamed in agony again.

"Turn your fragging persec off! Fragging stupid voltage shit. Frag!" Iskomo twisted and shook himself violently. "Turn it off! I told you that shit shorts my connection!"

"I'm sorry!" Sarah deactivated her persec, reaching down for Iskomo again. He flinched away, then slowly nodded at Sarah to help him up. "You need a specialist!" she gasped as she saw his destroyed hand. "Where are your fingers?"

"In him," Iskomo groaned. He was heavy and Sarah struggled to keep him balanced. "Forget it, just get help. I'm still shorted out, you need to."

"Who do I contact?" Sarah shifted Iskomo into a chair.

"Just anyone at O.M.T." Iskomo leaned back in the chair, nearly tipping it over. "Ask for McCavern, or Neals, anybody. Tell them Iskomo three-nine-nine-six! Are you writing this down?" Iskomo yelled so loud he was spitting. "Three-nine-nine-six!"

"Got it!" Iskomo heard Sarah announce as his world turned black.

6

"Getting an informant to call in. You might be losing your touch."

Iskomo opened his eyes. He was lying on a medical bed, and an expensive one at that. Rows of air-filled tubes formed the mattress, cycling heated air throughout them to keep him comfortable. He looked over to the voice, seeing Neals sitting beside him.

"McCavern sends his excuses," Neals continued. "How are you feeling Iskomo?"

"Like shit," Iskomo scratched an itch on his chin, recoiling at the sensation of the cold ceramic that touched his face. He held his hand away from him, inspecting it. He sat up, shaking his arm as if it would somehow dislodge the casing. "They aug'd it?"

"Yeah."

"Did you try to explain?"

"I wasn't here," Neals said bluntly. "The grafters saw you were on O.M.T. policy and just went with the best. They didn't realise you were bio-lined."

"Right. What else did they do?"

"They repaired some bruising to your chest and lungs and did a flush of the toxins in your system. As far as I know that was it."

"Explains why the hangover is gone." Iskomo studied his artificial hand again, sighing deeply. "Was only this morning I blew my earnings on getting my hands properly repaired organically. Shit." He checked his other hand, breathing a sigh of relief when it was still his original.

"I must admit you're taking this well," Neals observed. His hands shifted outside of Iskomo's vision.

"Must be the drugs. My self diagnostics is reporting I have quite a cocktail happening in my bloodstream." Iskomo checked over himself some more, trying to recall the last events he could remember. "The girl, where is she?"

"Detained. I thought I had seen hysterical before but this was a whole new level." Neals laughed. "McCavern pushed her through to incentives to get a statement underway. What's the action?"

Iskomo stared at Neals for a moment. "I know you would have already dug into the report."

"Yeah. I did." Neals admitted. "I was curious."

"Well, as you no doubt saw, it's open and shut. I found the attacker. Some courier who got hold of O.M.T. attire and harassed a skin model."

"What about the docker laying dead on her floor?"

"I'm going to look into that," Iskomo sat himself up. "Was any of it salvageable?"

"No. You wrecked his braincage pretty entirely."

"I knew it was a mistake." Iskomo laughed at himself. "But frag man, felt so good after the ass kicking I got."

"Stop doing that. Don't say it was a mistake again," warned Neals. "That would be two in as many days. Flashing badges, destroying potential evidence. Frag Iskomo, get it together."

Iskomo sighed again. "Well. I guess thanks for the visit. Were you in the area?"

Neals nodded. "My own investigation. Informant claims some Blackhat boasted about designing a backdoor into one of O.M.T.'s subsidiaries. Informant gets zero'd. I'm here for the scrubbers."

"Good luck with that," Iskomo sat up on the bed and swung his legs over the side. up from the bed. "Where are my clothes?"

"In the incinerator. Iskomo, they were bad man. Clothes shouldn't be... crusty."

"You torched them?"

"Course' I didn't. Frag Iskomo, you can't smell them?" Neals pointed to a silver container beneath Iskomo's bed. "At least have a shower before you go."

"Later," Iskomo looked at Neals and shrugged. "Maybe it'll rain on my way over and I'll spend some time in it." He dressed himself as Neals averted his eyes. "I better get back to it, especially if Sarah is causing trouble like you said. Catch up with you later? I know a good bar."

"Fragging hell," Neals laughed. "They flush your systems and you're already planning on loading up again." He stood up himself and accompanied Iskomo out of the room. "Maybe wait until the drugs wear off before adding more toxins. Sorry about the hand, but give it time, you may end up liking it."

Iskomo nodded and parted ways with Neals. He followed the displays leading to the exit of the ward and accessed his internal link to the Society. In his vision, an imposed display of options floated. Iskomo always preferred to access the Society using the bare surface level. Deep logging never sat well with him. The thought of submerging himself into an entirely virtual world while his physical body lay helpless was an exercise in vulnerability. He would happily accept the barebone holo-renders of pop-ups and flat surface pages if it meant he could be aware of his surroundings. That, and another reason.

After logging another rideshare, Iskomo entered the O.M.T. building towards the personnel area for the second time that day. He passed the smudge on the wall he left earlier, making his way to the incentives department. He could hear Sarah's outbursts of anger as he approached. The girl sure had a set of lungs on her. He paused before the door to where the yelling came from, taking a deep breath. He moved his pda to the door scanner and stopped when he heard a loud crash inside the room. Iskomo took another deep breath, grimaced, and swiped the scanner.

"Iskomo!" the Incentives tech cried out when he saw him enter. "Take your informant, please!" He scurried out of the room without waiting for a response.

"Iskomo?" Sarah stood there, panting heavily. She brushed some sweat away from her forehead, visibly exhausted. "Wait is that your name? I thought that was some zero code for you agents."

"How are you doing?" Iskomo walked into the room and sat the table upright. He placed one of the chairs behind it and sat down. The Incentive rooms used hard copy furniture, not the holographic suite. It made the incentives system more *physical*.

"Answer my question!" Sarah clenched her fists. "No one has been answering me. About anything! Where's the respect? I know a million casters who would love a description of how the O.M.T. has treated me!"

"Sit down," Iskomo kept his voice calm. "You don't want to making threats here." He waited as she succumbed and sat herself on the chair opposite him. "People call me Iskomo."

"You said it was Peter." Sarah crossed her arms.

"It's a tag. Who the frag cares. You go around telling everyone you're TG Boston? Give me a break. I just got my ass kicked for you."

Sarah nodded. She winced when Iskomo had used her online username, but didn't give away any other emotions. "Why am I here? What the frag is going on?"

"Easy one first. Oh, and I'm fine by the way, cheers for asking," Iskomo scoffed. "You were brought here for the recant."

"I'm not doing it."

"Yeah. I hoped you'd say that. I don't care about it anymore either," Iskomo quipped back.

Sarah's eyebrows raised. "What?"

"I'm serious, forget the recant. I can't close this case yet."

"Cause of the docker?"

"Yes. I don't know what that was about yet. But I'm going to find out."

"Why though? This morning you couldn't wait to wipe yourself off this case." Sarah rested back on the chair. "Oh wow, your hand."

"Forget it," Iskomo dismissed it. "Ask me again when the surgical drugs wear off. Are you still one hundred percent sure the man who attacked you yesterday wasn't the same one who got your roommate?"

"You're drugged right now? How can you even focus on this?"

"It's just emotion dampening, doesn't affect my logic. Answer my question? Different people yes?"

"Absolutely."

"Yet the footage put that courier Alcanter in the same place. What enemies have you made recently? No bullshit this time."

"I haven't!" Sarah's face returned to a scowl. "I haven't done anything differently to what I've normally done."

"You pissed off someone, enough to get them to pose as O.M.T. and now it's cost me my hand."

"Oh I see," Sarah bit back. "It is about your hand. Why don't you go frag yourself. I asked for help. I got none. I didn't think it would blow up like this."

"Alright," Iskomo held his hands up in front of him. "Calm down. I just want to get as much as I can. Properly, this time. I think there is an actual situation here."

"Can't you flush your system of the drugs? You're being, like, really weird. It's freaking me out."

"No. I am pissed about this hand. I just can't act on it while affected. I think I should let the dampeners go a bit longer." Iskomo tapped his ceramic hand with the other. "And people wonder why I drink."

Sarah sat silently staring at Iskomo. He didn't appear to notice.

"I was thinking about that docker," Iskomo continued. He looked at Sarah who continued to sit quietly. "I've seen witness silence jobs before. Brutes like that either hired or hacked to zero someone."

"Ok?" Sarah finally spoke.

"It's always a single directive when coded. Zero such and such," Iskomo kept eye contact with Sarah, hoping she was following with what he was saying. "This docker, he didn't even register you. He went for me. I was the target."

"So, do you check his systems? I don't know what you're dribbling about."

"Can't. Destroyed his brain cage too much for the scrubbers," Iskomo shrugged. "I'm saying I've seen informants get zero'd during open cases. Takes a lot to distract a hacked from the reprogram. This was for me. Now it could be related to something else, but I doubt it. Someone knows I'm on this investigation and tried zero me."

"What? You sound like there's some big conspiracy or something," Sarah was sceptical.

"Look around you at the world we live in. Everything is a big conspiracy."

Sarah put her face in her hands. "I can't take you seriously when you've just admitted you're loaded. You sure it doesn't affect your logic?"

"Oh, absolutely."

"It does?"

"It does not."

Another groan escaped Sarah's lips. "Alright then, conspiracy?"

"Conspiracy."

Sarah let out a small scream of frustration. "So what are you going to do?"

"A lot of things, all technical stuff. But from now on I think it's safe to assume we're both targeted."

Sarah rolled her eyes. "You're saying we should stick together?"

Iskomo shrugged. "I'm saying you should stay here."

"Frag that. I've seen how that turns out. Let's just make it more convenient for them shall we? The little loose end in one easy, inescapable location." Sarah made air quotation marks with her hands as she spoke.

"It's for your protection. You know I'm right." Iskomo put it bluntly.

"Whatever. I was worried you were going to drag me around all day. What's the next step then?"

"You'll be fine here. As for me, I know someone over at Titan Sec. I'll see where he's at regarding Alcanter's scrub. Easiest thing at the moment to do."

"Easiest? Forgive me," Sarah interrupted. "But you don't seem to be taking this very seriously."

"Oh I am. I just know to work smarter, not harder."

"Just like the O.M.T. adverts." Sarah observed. She paused and her facial expression got softer. "I know, I know. The drugs. I'm glad you're ok, for what it's worth."

"No problem," Iskomo wasn't sure what to say. "I'll go source that now." He stood up and made for the door. He felt a sense of accomplishment forming within himself. "I think the drugs are wearing off."

"Can't you just log on and get your guy to send you the files? And just purge in here, I don't mind."

"Not in these rooms, they have the signal safeguards. Shuts out certain applications and programs." Iskomo informed her as he swiped his pda again.

"You sure? I've been recording all this and backing it up to my home storage."

"What?"

"I just think footage of O.M.T. agents working under the influence might come in handy one day."

Iskomo stopped. "You have Society access? In here?" When Sarah nodded he quickly typed up a test memo package using his internal Society ports and tried sending it to his private account. The holographic pop up window in his vision flashed the word sent. "Frag!" Iskomo cursed and opened a direct line to McCavern, all formats of image, audio and text to get his attention. "McCavern! Lock down the safeguards on the Incentive rooms!"

"What the," McCavern slowly asked before Iskomo heard a flurry of frenzied button taps. Within seconds Iskomo's feed was cut and his link to the Society disabled. The windows and graphics where he could browse and explore replaced with a static O.M.T. acknowledgement image.

"I'm booted," Sarah said aloud. She looked at Iskomo. "Was I not supposed to get Society in here?"

"No. These are closed offices, no networks in or out."

"Then why could I?"

"Either someone in the tech department fragged up, or," Iskomo remembered his interaction with Rory Alcanter, "someone was watching."

"That's..." Sarah began.

"Shut it," Iskomo snapped. He paced the room, muttering aloud. "How did they know the exact room? Need to check the logs. Yes."

"Are you alright?" Sarah asked him, puzzled at his actions. "Is this still the surgical drugs?"

"Hmm? Yeah. No! Not the drugs, yeah I'm alright. It's called thinking aloud. Try it sometime."

"Wait. Do they know where I am?"

Iskomo stopped and clicked his fingers. The metal of his fingertips sparked and the clang echoed around the small room, giving Iskomo a jump. "Frag! Forgot about that." He muttered and took a second to inspect his augmented hand again, checking for damage. "You were uploading data to your home storage?"

"I said that, don't you..."

"That's how they found the room," Iskomo nearly clicked his fingers again but stopped himself. "I have to go," Iskomo turned and quickly walked out the room, ignoring Sarah's angry calls behind him as she was left behind, the door closing silencing her again.

His pace quickened as he rounded corners and hallways towards McCavern's office. He nearly threw his pda at the door swipe panel in his rush to get inside.

"Iskomo! What the frag was that?" McCavern had all four Society ports jacked into his skull and was typing furiously onto his desk.

"We got breached, you got a source?"

"It's layered, all traces keep looping back to in-house." McCavern never took his gaze from his monitors, his red eye flickering with data processing.

"Has a Dagesh from Titan Security sent over anything yet?" Iskomo asked, hoping McCavern hadn't dived fully yet.

"No, shall I request?"

"Yes, they had a breach this morning too, they were sending a data packet once they decrypted."

McCavern's typing paused and his fingers lifted up off the desk. "That is a lot of processing," he made an almost sigh sound. "Can't spare the port I'm at max."

"So dive," Iskomo suggested. Before the words had escaped his lips McCavern's body had slumped and Iskomo knew he was under. Iskomo sat himself down in the other chair and reconnected his Society access.

Neals, your informant scrubber about the backdoor, any luck? Iskomo penned the message without formality and sent it.

Just collected. You need a link? The reply was instant.

O.M.T. had a breach, get it back here now. Hardcopy only. Iskomo feared sending it online would only lead to more disasters.

What? On my way!

McCavern came out of his Society dive and commenced his typing again. "Titan Sec. isn't releasing the data yet."

"Fragging hell," Iskomo muttered.

"Usual legal blockers. I don't have time to brute force my way in. It involves your assignment?" McCavern unplugged one of his head jacks.

"Yes. They also had a signal breach. I'm thinking it's related."

"Thought that was done, you asked for the security feeds earlier."

"That was before..."

"Before the incident at Blackwell's apartment." McCavern finished Iskomo's sentence. "Right. You get the recant yet?"

Iskomo hesitated. "Not yet. This is more pressing."

McCavern gave a small grunt in agreement. "Still looping back to us." He pulled out the remaining three jacks from the side of his head. "Hard wired is compromised. I'm switching to wireless. I have to log this breach. Was there anything else?"

"I've got Neals returning. He mentioned a possible backdoor breach to our systems."

McCavern didn't respond. Iskomo realised he was in a dive again, possibly logging the attack. A small twist of his head let Iskomo know he was back. "Seems a bit obvious doesn't it?"

"Maybe it's just luck," Iskomo offered. "He said it was through one of the subsidiaries."

"I remember when hackers were good at what they did. Now they're all one trick proxies. They just reuse the same programs for everything. Real creatures of habit," McCavern laughed. Iskomo sat quietly, waiting for him to continue. "Come on. This," McCavern pointed at his terminal with the tracer program still running, "this is skill. Whoever breached wouldn't be sloppy about loose ends. If anything, it's a designed distraction. I guarantee whatever Neals has will be a red herring."

Iskomo stroked his chin, "If it is a red herring as you say, that does still mean it is connected, somehow."

McCavern groaned and minimised the screen. "You know what I mean. Not worth pursuing." McCavern became distracted again with his red eye flickering.

"Found something?" Iskomo was leaning forward in his chair.

"Just an alert for some potential property damage from your informant. She's trashing the Incentive room. With this breach, I think I have to pass this up."

Iskomo gritted his teeth. "What? No."

"It's procedure."

"This is my informant and my case, you can't send it up the line."

"You've never had a problem with that before," McCavern dryly stated. "You'll retain the earnings."

"They attacked *me*," Iskomo stressed the word. "I got a feeling this is big."

"All the more reason to pass it upwards." McCavern plugged another Society jack into his skull. "Activate Incentive room 13R sedative system. I need all your files."

"Come on McCavern," Iskomo stood up. "You're going to do this to me?"

"It's done. Transfer them over." McCavern opened a wireless link between them and downloaded all of Iskomo's notes and pda entries from the case.

"Don't feel right," Iskomo muttered. "Not this time."

"Worry about it later," McCavern turned and activated the full size wall display. "You've got your next assignment."

7

"Jody Banks, development assistant at Avery. Credentials cleared," Iskomo read aloud while scrolling the details on his pda, shifting uncomfortably in his seat. It didn't list much about the claim, just that Jody was scared enough to request a private audience with an agent.

"They do Fuzion card, yeah?" the driver of the rideshare quipped from behind his plexiglass barrier.

"Oh, so now you're listening?" Iskomo didn't attempt to hide the irritation in his voice. "You clearly weren't when I told you to keep to a land tariff."

"Sky is faster, cheaper. You end up saving more. I do it to please my customers."

"Frag off. You want to please your customers? Then listen to what they say."

"Well, the next customer is up here anyway, above street pickup." The driver gave a lazy shrug.

Iskomo groaned, "Give you double if you skip it."

"My system already gave the confirmation."

"Offer still stands."

The driver laughed softly, "You already paying less with air tariff. And I'm starting to think you fossils don't quite understand the idea."

"Oh I get it," Iskomo began but was cut off.

"Ride-share. Not some solo escort service. Share the ride, save the earth, yadda, yadda, yadda."

Iskomo ignored the driver and refocused on his pda. He became distracted as the vehicle approached a large residential skyscraper. It had the hallmarks of being pre-mass-produced era with its sloping, silver design. Care had gone into keeping it restored. Small gardens filled every terrace, each with its own vehicle port. The rideshare continued climbing higher. Iskomo swapped his focus between his pda and the wall of apartments beside him, too nervous to look out his own passenger window at the height they had climbed. He shifted over when he felt the vehicle touch down, making room for the next passenger. He decided to return to his pda, his mind well aware of the distant ground outside his door.

"Corners of East three and Delmont," the feminine voice beside him informed the driver.

"Already uploaded," the driver chirped back.

Iskomo steadied himself as the vehicle lurched upwards, spun and coasted towards the Delmont sector. "Hey what the frag!" he called to the driver.

"Taking her to her destination." There was a hint of vengeful joy in the driver's flat answer.

"I was first passenger," argued Iskomo. "You drop travellers in the order they..." Iskomo felt like throwing his hands up in the air, bewildered at what was occurring. He almost did, but feared it would rock the vehicle further.

"It be like you said, you paying double for your fare."

"That was if you... frag it!" Iskomo slumped back in his seat and looked at the passenger beside him. She was possibly of an age circling twenty, it was hard to tell these days. Her hair was done up in a giant neon pink bow, with smaller pigtails hanging from underneath the large folds of hair. Her face was covered in green and blue cyber tattoos. The ones resembling old electrical circuit designs. Iskomo found himself staring too long at the oddity of it all. She kept facing forward but her eyes drifted to notice him.

"You're trying to figure it out." she said.

"Hmm?" Iskomo didn't like being that obvious.

"You're looking at me, wondering how *someone* who looks like me lives in a place like this. Am I right?"

"I just don't like heights. At least, not in a vehicle. That feeling of nothing beneath you."

"Nice try. But I can tell. It's my job to tell. I'm lead reporter at Bold-inc. News," she gave him a smile and pulled out a business holo-card from her black corset top. "Tiffany Brass."

Iskomo politely took the holo-card and read it. "Boldinc?" He knew the brand.

"Are you one of our billion subscribers?" asked Tiffany.

"I am," the driver spoke up. "Very big fan. Your ride's on me."

Tiffany squealed and gave a small clap. "Always nice to meet a fan." She returned to Iskomo. "How about you? I wouldn't mind some one on one time with you."

Iskomo and the driver scoffed in unison. Tiffany pulled back, confused.

"No, I'm not a subscriber, and no, not interested," Iskomo said.

"Oh but come on," Tiffany's voice turned into a spoiled child whining. "I want to do a piece about O.M.T. and their agents. Just one little, itty, bitty interview?"

"No," Iskomo put it firmly. "And you know what? Don't call yourself a reporter. You think that's journalism what you're doing? I see it on the networks, these so called 'articles'. Every time I go onto the Society I see them, but it isn't news. Frag no. You and everyone else don't even write them anymore. It's just crowd sourced from everywhere. Fragging posts and clips and shit from other people that you," he pointed angrily at Tiffany, "paste together in some fragging holo slide show bullshit and count the views."

"What the frag," Tiffany looked ready to slap Iskomo.

"No one gives a shit about the top twenty holofeeds about being single in Lower Brisbane."

"I do," the driver tried to join.

"Typical fossil, we have billions of subscribers! Billions! And guess what, they're all watching me livestream this right now." Tiffany snatched the card back.

Iskomo's pda made an alert for an incoming message.

"Probably your boss," Tiffany seethed. "Telling you you're fired!"

"Shut up," Iskomo said and tried unlocking his pda screen. He felt his stomach turn and a sudden feeling of weightlessness. The vehicles engines went quiet and it leaned heavily to its right. Iskomo slid in his chair with the slope bumping into Tiffany. He checked and saw the driver had slumped in his seat as the car began to free fall. Tiffany gripped the seat and began screaming wildly into Iskomo's ears.

Iskomo pulled himself back to the centre as the rideshare wobbled and spun. His stomach felt like it was constantly rising. Floors of the building beside them rushed upwards. Iskomo kicked at the plexiglass, balancing himself as the vehicle collected speed. He tried to open his door, finding it locked. The ground outside the windows rushed towards him. He punched at the plexiglass, his ceramic fist bursting a hole through it. He clawed at it. Tore away chunks. Tiffany vomited. Iskomo made a hole big enough to squeeze his upper torso through and lunged for the vehicle's ignition button. He strained, reaching further as he was out of range to touch it. He thought he could see people's faces on the street below. He stretched again, this time tapping the button.

The engine kicked into life and instantly dampeners slowed their descent. The inertia of the deceleration dug the plexiglass hole into Iskomo's back. Outside, he could see they were two stories off the ground. The rideshare drifted lower, at a much safer pace and touched down in an emergency lane. Iskomo realised he was holding his breath and exhaled. He took a deep breath, then emptied his stomach into the driver's cabin.

Wiping the bile from his mouth, he caught the driver's eyes watching him. Body still slumped, but the eyes following Iskomo as he shifted to clear himself of the plexiglass. Iskomo pulled himself into the front and bent his head down, face to face with the driver.

"You in there?" Iskomo asked.

"Help me," the driver whimpered back, unable to move anything but his face.

"Not talking to you," Iskomo pointed at the driver. "Talking to whoever else is in there, piggybacking your skull. Still watching?"

The driver groaned and his eyes rolled back. When they returned, they had lost the frantic searching and became still and focused.

"There you are," Iskomo almost grinned. "I'm going to find you."

The driver remained silent, staring coldly at Iskomo. Iskomo switched to his internal network, trying a line to McCavern.

"He can't help you," the driver finally spoke.

"So you're monitoring O.M.T. lines too. Just gave yourself away," said Iskomo.

"You have nothing."

"I have a shit sense of being in the right place at wrong times. Who was the target here? The neon brat?"

"You. Her livestream just made it easier to find you."

"Only cowards hide behind proxies."

"You're a coward behind a badge."

"I at least face my enemies head on. Not rely on some innocent third party. Why don't you just get into your actual targets head itself? Some sick game?"

"I don't have to explain anything to you."

"Yet here you are, just chatting away."

"That's because some things take time. You think its all some big conspiracy? It's not. I'm nobody. I say we both just walk away. Just don't get in my way anymore and I'll stop needing to zero you."

"What's your aim here?"

"Why would I tell you that? And what does it matter? People die all the time, daily, hourly. I made a mistake and it got out of hand. Doesn't matter. From what I can see you have literally nothing to find me with."

"Oh I'll find you," Iskomo held up his ceramic hand. "You took this from me."

"Then I'll just need to contain you. This could work to my favour actually."

Iskomo's internal display suddenly switched on, popping up an overlay into his vision to reveal his pda upload was complete. He turned around in the front seat, seeing Tiffany sitting frozen with a blank expression, Iskomo's pda in her hands.

"You motherfragger," Iskomo sneered.

"Do you know how pesticides used to work?" the driver's throat looked clenched.

"Chemicals," Iskomo answered.

"Yes. More like, they attacked the nervous system." Each word was becoming more strained. "Made the poor creature spasm uncontrollably until they died of exhaustion."

"You claiming to be some sort of pest removal?"

"Keep watching," the veins in the driver's neck bulged. His eyes watered and grew red. "Little pulses of electricity, enough for muscle control. Let the pulse become a steady stream and the muscles don't relax. It's the same idea. Nice talking to you."

"Listen here-" Iskomo stopped as the driver went into full body convulsions. He grabbed at him with his ceramic hands and tried to steady him. Iskomo could hear the laboured breaths as the driver's neck tightened itself more. "I'm sorry," he told the driver as he closed his fist and hit the back of the drivers head. Knocked out, the driver continued to spasm to Iskomo's horror. The driver's face turned a dark shade of purple, veins bulging in his neck that looked ready to burst through the stretched skin of the neck. The drivers body gave one final violent spasm and went limp.

Iskomo turned back to the rear passenger seat, discovering it empty. He searched the surrounding area from his seat finding Tiffany Brass standing in the express lane of the street. She held Iskomo's pda to her chest, winking at him as the automated delivery truck slammed into her.

8

"It's been a while since I'd seen a proper shit show." Neals said. "Honestly I'm truly amazed you haven't been scrubbed from the roster yet."

"Probably because no one is aware yet,' Iskomo revealed. He stood against the rideshare's door, watching the clean up progress. Organic waste employee's, who now were more hardware than flesh, worked around the scene. Ground traffic was diverted up and over, the under-carriages of the unmanned vehicles a little too close for Iskomo's liking. One worker, unbothered by the rush of vehicles above him continued to vacuum up the blood that stretched down the lane. Pausing momentarily to screenshot his progress with his artificial eyes. Iskomo wondered how many media sites would be sharing the images later as countless visitors claimed Tiffany Brass was their personal hero.

"How do you figure?"

Iskomo pointed at the remains of the reporter, now a heap of blood soaked flesh and metallic parts, as it passed them into an organic waste truck. "Somewhere in that mess is my pda."

"Just log in through your systems. They need to know."

"Oh they know," Iskomo sighed. "Metro will have released reports on the situation already. What more is there?"

"Your explanation for one. You really need to start using the company wetware."

"I like the old school stuff. I don't like having my senses turned off."

"Yeah, yeah. Heard it all before. If you'd get off your ass and get patched you'd see the system has really improved."

Iskomo grumbled beneath his breath. He searched for a way out of it. "I'll fill the report later, right now I need to stay on track. Mind or-ganising me a ride to the Avery offices?"

"That's been recalled," Neals said.

"What? Why? Because of this?" Iskomo pointed at the scene before them.

"You're talking about the Jody Banks inquiry?"

"The one I was assigned, yes."

"Ain't no Jody Banks anymore, so ain't no inquiry."

"Fragging hell," cursed Iskomo. "Today just keeps getting more and more fragged."

"I'll take you back to H.Q. You can get patched, submit whatever the hell happened here and move on like normal."

Iskomo shook his head. "No. Something is going on. I need to find out what happened to Jody Banks, see if it's connected."

"McCavern said you were sliding. Banks has been resolved and closed by Metro. They caught the guy, full suite of evidence including a confession."

"I'm not sliding. This is the work of one person."

"You're saying a serial killer?" Neals stifled a laugh. "Are you listening to me Iskomo? They caught the mark. I heard you even caught yours. I really think you need a check-up, something has crossed inside your head."

"Who then? Who did they catch?"

"Some guy out of the northern blocks. Dispute over owed money they reported."

"Neals, just listen. The driver," Iskomo motioned to the vehicle with his arms crossed. "He got brainjacked. I was talking to someone. He said he was going to contain me."

"The driver?" Neals walked over to the truck holding the bodies and pointed at the corpse. "Doesn't have any gear in his throat. Even if hacked, there's no way to stimulate the vocal cords to actually have a conversation with someone in reality."

"Neals, I'm telling you," Iskomo was cut short as Neals held up a finger. "What is it?"

"You didn't get the alert too?" Neals became suddenly serious. He looked around the area and stared at a ground traffic security camera on the opposite side of the road lanes. "Footage has been forwarded from that vidfeed, a loop of you hitting the driver in the back of the head."

"I was trying to knock him out. I thought it may cut the hacker's control to the muscles."

"This doesn't look good," Neals was grim.

"Forward it to me," Iskomo requested. He accessed his internal mail system and waited.

"Keep getting errors," Neals sighed, then smacked Iskomo with the back of his hand. "You're fragging out of date. I keep saying that."

"Never affected compatibility before."

"Well it does now. This is bad Iskomo. This is the kind of attention O.M.T. hates."

"I know."

"What did you say earlier? You were untouchable?"

"I know what I said," Iskomo said, his voice laced with anger.

"Still, looking at this from a professional viewpoint. You might be lucky yet. I hate to say it, but I may agree with you."

"About what?" asked Iskomo.

"For this to be leaked so quickly. Smells like a plant."

"Someone is a bit too eager to frame me."

Neals nodded. "Had a little shit a few years ago try the same to me."

"If H.Q. have got this then I've got no choice now but to go back and give my statement." Iskomo stood up from the rideshare. "Would that camera pick up audio?"

"From over there? Doubtful. What are you thinking?"

"Just feels like it was done to stop me from following up on Jody Banks. I'm wondering if they heard me talking about it." Iskomo found himself staring at the camera.

"I said I was starting to agree, but let's take it easy with the full-blown paranoia hey?" Neals walked Iskomo to another waiting rideshare. "We need to get back."

"Did you see Blackwell when you were there?" Iskomo wasn't sure why he asked.

"No. I went straight to McCavern expecting you to be there too. He told me it was moved up."

"Yeah they took it off me. Do you have your data on that breach you mentioned?"

"Ah," Neals frowned. "I was told not to provide it to you."

"Come on Neals, help me out. I'm looking for any possible link here."

"Well it's too late now anyway. The breach in the sub-branch got fixed."

"When?"

"Before all this happened, therefore, not related." Neals opened the door for Iskomo, climbing into the rideshare after him.

"Then what's the harm?" Iskomo asked. He watched the driver in front of them carefully. "Your Society access secure?"

The driver turned around, surprised. "Excuse me?"

"Your link to the Society. All your defences up to date?" Iskomo demanded an answer.

"I drive a rideshare, you do the math." The driver turned back around.

"I'm not going anywhere in this," Iskomo announced, reaching for the door. The Rideshare lurched up a small distance from the ground and began shifting to its right. "Motherfragger," cursed Iskomo. He watched helplessly as an organic waste worker directed the driver to merge back into the flowing traffic. Seamlessly, the vehicle entered the diverted path, passing over the disabled vehicles below before setting down. "Keep it on the ground," ordered Iskomo.

"Off ground and I can get you to O.M.T. in half the time," the driver suggested.

"Fragging hell, they're all the fragging same." Iskomo leaned forward in his seat, placing his ceramic hand on the plexiglass for the driver to see. "Keep on the ground or I'll make it my personal mission to rid the world of rideshares."

"I can only take requests from the paying customer."

"Relax Iskomo," Neals assured him. "Ground tariff is fine. Thank you."

The rideshare glided back down to the ground roads and Iskomo let out a deep breath.

"You're certain your driver was brainjacked?"

"Been over this a million times. Yes. Whoever it was hacked the driver, sent us into a freefall and spoke to me. Tiffany Brass too."

"Spoke to her as well?' asked Neals.

"No, got brainjacked as well."

"She would have had the best security systems. I doubt she got brainjacked."

"She uploaded my pda to somewhere then walked into traffic. It's like going in circles whenever I talk to you." Iskomo sighed.

"Just get patched and you'll see for yourself, the new system is so fluid."

"I don't want to, alright?" Iskomo clenched his fists. "Every new patch requires constant fragging updates, new changes to the interface. I get the whole, keep up or be left behind." Iskomo saw Neals's expression on his face. "And I ain't no fossil either. I just think being left behind isn't that big a deal anymore."

"Like it or not, it's a requirement of the job, remember?"

"Yeah well, I'll determine when it's done."

"With all that's happened you might not get to. What you said about last night, this shit today. Might be mandatory if you're to be kept on. It's not so bad, it's really secure now."

Iskomo continued to shake his head then paused. "What do you mean, now?"

"Ah, frag," cursed Neals.

Iskomo studied him harder. "The breach in the subsidiary. It was the department that compiled the new patch?"

"Iskomo…"

"Frag you! Take me there now!" Iskomo pointed at Neals accusingly. "Investigator my arse. It isn't obvious to you that it is connected? Like I fragging said already!"

"You know, you've been a real asshole since the wife left you." Neals said it quietly, but the entire vehicle heard it.

"Don't you bring her into this," Iskomo warned through clenched teeth.

"But she is. Let me tell you what *this* investigator has noticed so far," Neals bit back. "Ever since your wife ran off you've spiralled. You come into work hungover everyday which means you've been finding the real stuff. At least synthetic alcohol doesn't leave you smelling like shit and looking like death the next morning. Every job you've had has been half-arsed, looking for the quick solution."

"A lot of agents do that," protested Iskomo.

"I ain't finished," said Neals. "What did you say this morning? Let me self-destruct the way I want to? A fight with a power loaded docker, that fragging rideshare back there? You're seeking it out man."

Iskomo sat silently, a hundred counter arguments ran inside his head. If only he could decide which one to use.

"Is it the skin model? Has she got you thinking you're all young again? Doing all this reckless shit?"

The question shocked Iskomo, blanking his thoughts. "What? Of course not!"

"I get if you're lonely. But it's got you all over the place."

"Frag off Neals!" Iskomo shoved him. "I have no interest in the brat apart from resolving the job!"

Neals shoved Iskomo back, "The job was passed to the higher ups! It's done."

The driver adjusted his mirror and called out, stammering, "No fighting between passengers!"

"Just give me the data," Iskomo ordered.

"No. And regardless, the transfer wouldn't work anyway with your outdated systems. You used that pda for everything." He gave Iskomo a final shove.

Iskomo considered returning it when he noticed the rideshare had stopped outside the Boldinc News building. "What the frag?"

The driver turned around and faced Neals. "Direct or b-card?"

"Direct," Neals answered.

"I thought we were going back the H.Q?" Iskomo asked as Neals exited the vehicle.

"We have," Neals looked confused at Iskomo's question. "Let's go inside and get to McCavern. This report can't be delayed any longer."

"Where are we?" Iskomo asked the driver instead.

"At your destination, O.M.T. corporation building, level two."

"Do you have global positioning?" Iskomo asked. There was no indication of it in the front console of the vehicle.

The driver chuckled nervously. "Of course? Internal only though."

Iskomo hesitantly got out of the vehicle and stared at the Boldinc. News logo that covered the building. It flashed different shades of neon colours, then morphed into a dot point system of the day's top stories.

"Hurry up," Neals demanded as he walked towards the entrance.

Iskomo tried to access his link to the Society. If he could find a quick GPS service to download he'd give himself more answers. The menu popped up overlaying in his vision, asking for his credentials. The choice was given, password or bio-signature, his preferred. He stopped himself before accepting it, a cold sweat forming on him. "Are we at O.M.T.?"

Neals marched back to where Iskomo stood on the sidewalk. "You're really this against getting a patch? Get it done and I'll buy your alcohol tonight."

"I think I'm being brainjacked," Iskomo said softly. He kept his body movements still, debating whether running a sudden diagnostic on his systems would alert the intruder.

"Get inside then, quickly. Hopefully your incompatible systems buy us some time." Neals ushered Iskomo in through the doors and walked past the front reception terminals.

"Neals?" Iskomo watched as Neals continued towards the hallways further into the building. Red lights began blinking on the roof and Iskomo could hear security systems activating from behind the walls.

Neals turned around and began walking back towards Iskomo. "Nearly there." He walked away from the secure area, past the terminals again towards an open meeting space. Tables lay around the area set up for a function. "McCavern must be out, we'll just wait here in his office." Neals said and sat down at one of the tables that was set up with cutlery. A small holo display in the centre of the table rotated the words *reserved*.

"It's you!" an unfamiliar voice called across the foyer.

Iskomo turned to see another punk styled journalist approaching him. Fishnet stockings, black bands and bright neon green hair spiked into a mohawk. She pointed at Iskomo and Iskomo heard the flickering of her eyes taking pictures rapidly. Iskomo looked back over at Neals, sitting at the table silently. "It's not me," he realised. He backed away from the reporter and took a seat beside Neals. "Neals, shut down your link right now."

"Hey! Don't ignore me!" the reporter followed Iskomo to the table. "Do you have any comments regarding Miss Brass? Footage shows you were with her before the accident."

"Ah McCavern," Neals greeted the reporter. "How do we fix this mess?"

The reporter ignored Neals, continuing to record Iskomo. Iskomo shook Neals's shoulder. "Cut your link!"

Neals didn't acknowledge the nudge. He reached onto the table setting and picked up a knife. "Sounds simple enough." He turned to Iskomo. "See it's a really simple procedure. Just got to place the Patch-stim into your neck port. It'll begin the auto-update."

"Wait," Iskomo grabbed hold of Neals hand with the knife, being careful not to let his ceramic strength of that one crush Neal's wrist.

Neals grunted and became angry. "We've been over this. You heard McCavern! It's in your best interest!" He struggled to free himself from Iskomo's grip.

"Are you getting this?" Iskomo shouted at the reporter. "Save it! It's O.M.T. evidence!"

The reporter's eyes had rolled back, her mouth hanging open.

Iskomo continued to hold Neals arm down with his grip. *Think frag it!* he demanded himself. The whole situation reminded him of the freefall in the rideshare. He heard McCavern's voice in his head, *one trick proxies, always the same programs.* Iskomo checked his internal clock. As he suspected, roughly an hour had passed since the rideshare driver hack. If McCavern's biases were correct, Iskomo was dealing with an amateur.

Iskomo searched for an exit. The reporter remained in her trance, something Iskomo was thankful for. Neals continued to struggle, forcing Iskomo to use both his hands to stop from being struck. Red security lights began to blink on the roof again, alerting Iskomo the need for urgency.

Iskomo heaved Neals away from him. He then followed it up by flipping the table towards Neals in an attempt to slow him. Iskomo grabbed the reporter, unholstering his gun and holding it to her head. "Don't move or I'll kill McCavern!"

"You've lost your damn mind Iskomo!" Neals yelled. "Now you're truly fragged."

The reporter came out of her trance and noticed the gun pressed against her head. She screamed then recomposed herself. "This just in, I'm being held at gunpoint in a hostage situation inside our own offices. Subscribe for more details."

Iskomo saw panels in the roof open and large security guns hang down from them. They swivelled as they searched for a lock on their target. Fifty percent of the time they held non-lethal rounds, but Iskomo decided not to find out. He shoved the reporter towards Neals and ran for the exit.

9

"Where the frag is Iskomo? Who the frag are you?"

"Miss Blackwell, for the last time, please calm down," the corporate suit asked her. "As soon as you make your recant, you are free to go."

"I want to see that bastard!" she screamed again. It had felt like hours since Iskomo had left her. After she had successfully trashed the first room she had been left in she was moved to another. In her anger she set about vandalising that one too. The third room they had shifted her to contained no furniture or observation windows. The camera in the corner protected by two layers of security mesh.

"Your case was moved up to a higher tier," the suit explained. "Your original investigator has been assigned a new case."

"That's bullshit," Sarah tapped the side of her head. "I signed up for hourly progress reports! I haven't had one since I've been here!"

"On behalf of O.M.T. I apologise for our investigators lack of communication. However as stated before, they have been reassigned and are no longer contractually obliged to continue the update feature." The man expressed himself with no emotion.

"I want to see him. I don't know how many times I got to say that."

"Then provide your recant and you are free to go. You will be able to try locate him after you leave."

"I want to speak to him before I give any recant," Sarah seethed.

"Again, that won't be possible."

Sarah clenched her fists and screamed at the roof. "Frag off!" She wanted the whole floor to hear her.

"We can try this again after you calm down," the suited man turned and nodded at the camera. The door slid open and he walked through, breathing a sigh of relief.

Another hour and she was truly bored. After Iskomo had left the room her connection to the Society had been severed, yet she still tried to connect repeatedly. She scrolled through photos in her vision. Clothes she wanted, ideas for her shows. She had close to two thousand images of random things she wanted online, and only three images of Stephanie.

She loaded up some of the brain training games she once installed years ago. They all immediately asked for her details to which she denied. She searched through her installed systems for any form of entertainment, finding a forgotten puzzle game she had never played.

She made it through the tutorial easily enough, matching the required grids to the corresponding clues. It wasn't much but it was better than boredom. She started the main game and completed the first level, a simple grid of four cubes. She activated the continue option for the next level when the game froze. She wondered if the file was corrupt. A message popped up in her vision, overlaying the game.

You have disabled advertisements. Please enable advertisements to continue.

Sarah cursed and shut down the game. She tried her other systems, curious to how many of them relied on an active Society connection. Mailing systems and everything online was, obviously, disabled. She could still record video but was unable to upload it anywhere. She recorded a short one of herself explaining her situation, the lack of communication from O.M.T. and her plans on what to do next. She finished compiling the video and set it to play back to herself. The image was blocked with the O.M.T. logo, with a message warning it was now considered O.M.T. property.

She sat against the wall, her energy spent. Looking through more of her systems, she decided to clean out a cache of temporary files that were beginning to pile up. She hadn't noticed any slowing of functions but her head felt lighter after it completed. She continued exploring through the different systems, one by one. There was some adware hidden inside an avatar system that she removed, thankful that it wasn't her main avatar program. She arrived at the Persec folder and decided to open it.

The folder contained all of the same options her main home menu had. Activate, deactivate, reports. She tried the activate option and sighed when it failed to initialise. But so did the deactivate and reports options. She wondered if this was the O.M.T.'s brand of torture, making the majority of her programs become inaccessible. Sarah decided to pass the time by beginning a virtual storage restructure. She cut the contents of the Persec folder and placed them into the previous unused avatar folder. She began to rename the folder when she heard noises from behind the door. She quickly closed all her virtual file exploration.

The door to the room slid open and Sarah stood herself back up. She eyed the new man cautiously. He was clearly a techhead with the hardware installed on his face. Even with so much machinery the man looked tired and sick. "Are you here to rewind me?"

"Sarah Blackwell, you may call me McCavern," he remained in the doorway as he introduced himself. "As much as it would speed things up there are still laws and regulations against forced memory access."

"Are you a friend of Iskomo's?" Sarah recalled using the name when Iskomo had been bleeding out on her kitchen floor.

"His boss," McCavern attempted a smile. The skin that remained on his face almost seemed translucent. His electronic red eye was laser tight. "Technically I'm an Allocator, I sort through the informant tip lines and dispense the jobs."

"Where is Iskomo?"

"You've already been told this information. Iskomo is currently assigned to another case."

"You said you assign them? Make him take it again."

"The case was upgraded to a level beyond Iskomo. I'll let you in on a secret though. The higher ups really want this resolved and it's already taken too long. Provide a recant now and O.M.T. will compensate you."

Sarah considered it for a moment. "Do you know what I do? How much my cam shows make? How much I've lost being stuck in this room?"

"It will be considered. But we also point out you would be home already if you had provided the recant."

"You are a creepy motherfragger," said Sarah. "Anyone ever tell you that?"

"The recant, if you would."

"No," Sarah paced around the room. "Desperate you said? O.M.T. really can't handle a little bit of bad P.R.? Let me guess, my followers are asking where I am, and they're flooding O.M.T. servers looking. Am I right so far?" When he didn't respond she flashed him a small grin. "The last thing Iskomo said to me was to forget the recant. I ain't doing shit until I see him."

This time McCavern grinned. "You think Iskomo had your best interests in mind?" He entered the room, leaving the door open and turned to face the blank wall. His red eye began projecting a video onto it.

Sarah watched as a security camera footage began playing on the wall. Iskomo was sitting in an office opposite the man before her. She heard Iskomo curse and stand up. He kicked the chair away and continued talking to McCavern.

"Here," McCavern told her in person, pointing at the wall. The vidfeed showed Iskomo lean over on the table, asking for a triple rate. "He's being paid triple for this job. That's why he is trying to extend it."

It didn't add up in Sarah's mind. A moment ago she was being told it was no longer Iskomo's case anyway. She believed her followers were causing chaos online, but was also aware that the longer she remained stuck here the more her online presence would suffer. Without interaction with her audience, she would be forgotten quickly. She saw no other option of getting out of this room without providing the recant. If she truly did consider herself an actress, now was the time to prove it. "Fine," she scoffed, "I'll give the recant."

McCavern shut off the projection. "That's very smart. Whenever you're ready."

Sarah waited and shrugged. "Well?"

"Provide your recant. I will record it."

"Ugh, no," Sarah stated. "Remove whatever these program locks you have on me and I'll do it."

"If you wish to record it yourself that's fine," McCavern said. "The Society lock will not be removed though."

"Listen to me. I use an avatar in my shows with a unique signature key. A lot of my fans are hackers and the sort. You want a recant from me? Well it won't be worth anything unless it's posted from my authenticated account. They will spot a proxy a mile away."

McCavern considered the information. "I'll lift the Society lock on you, but only in your local programs to allow you access to your avatar signature key. You won't be able to connect to the greater Society network."

"That's fine," Sarah said. She moved closer to McCavern. "How do you unlock my files? Do you need to link a cable or something?"

McCavern's red eye flickered quickly. "No it's already done. Folders with any keywords relating to avatar have been made fully functional. Now set up and provide the recant."

Sarah had never felt so lucky. Knowing McCavern was following her access path she dove into her files. She found the folder still labelled from her obsolete avatar and opened it. McCavern hadn't reacted so she continued on. She located the activate program and enabled it.

"I'm transferring you a document to read for your recant," announced McCavern.

Sarah received the download alert and accepted, returning to her internal home screen. "Alright," she said as she took a deep breath. "Here goes nothing."

McCavern's eye flashed but he reacted slow. Sarah reached out for him with a quick movement, unable to help but grimace as she made her move. Her hand connected with McCavern's chest and his body immediately convulsed in a spasm. He let out a cry of agony and collapsed to the floor. He continued to shake violently when Sarah realised he had fallen onto her foot. She pulled it away from him, leaving him panting for breath.

"Iskomo hated it too," she told him. "Said it would short his connections."

Running out the door, she made her way down the hallway, trying to remember the different paths she had taken when forced into new rooms. Rounding a corner she narrowly dodged another O.M.T. agent. He began to call out but Sarah brushed his arm as she passed. He recoiled in pain, giving Sarah enough time to get plenty of distance in her sprint. She ran on, looking for any sign of an exit. The halls were windowless. Sarah imagined herself in the belly of some giant corporate beast. She jumped down a flight of stairs not pausing. Rushing past all manner of employees she did her best to avoid them. Every few would connect with her and cry out in agony. People ahead of her would turn around and see the commotion and its effect, getting clear of her path as she sprinted past.

She came down another set of stairs and began getting alerts from the Society. Her professional inbox was at max storage space and her website had been overloaded with traffic. Her private message system had thirteen messages, all from Iskomo. She ignored accessing them and focused on her escape. With her Society access returned she took it as a sign she was close to an exit.

Sarah descended another level. Rounding another corner she began passing windows. She looked outside as she ran, relieved to see she was now on a balcony level. Up ahead on her right were doors leading to an outside platform edged with gardens. Her legs began to ache as she reached it and left the interior. On a small pad at the end of the balcony a rideshare was dropping off two women in business suits. Sarah pushed herself for the final stretch, knocking the two women aside and dived into the open passenger door.

"Go!" She screamed.

10

"After some new tech?" the shop assistant was overly friendly. "You look like a guy who gets stuff done. How about some new legs to match that hand?" He whistled when he got a closer look at it. "That is some pretty legit hardware, let me show you our top line stuff."

Iskomo tried to back himself away from the crowding assistant. "Just after a personal data assistant. Nothing fancy."

The assistant frowned. "Really? Try the clearance rack, I guess. No one uses them anymore, are you a collector?"

"Can I just look?" Iskomo flashed an angry look at him. The assistant pointed towards a section labelled retro and walked away, greeting another customer.

He had managed to get clear of Boldinc. easily. Keeping to alleys and his eyes focused to the ground he had covered a few blocks on foot. He didn't try to access the Society. If he had been brainjacked the last thing he needed was giving whoever was watching his access keys. Without the connection, his GPS remained useless. He was in an unfamiliar area of the city. Between the buildings he had managed to identify the towering Technix Colonies just a few more blocks away. He had never been this close to the rival corporate giant.

Apart from the possible brainjack, Iskomo didn't concern himself too much about O.M.T. follow-up. He was one man in a city of billions, and there were always bigger concerns in the world of corporate business. He had a desire to know if he was officially fired yet. He wondered if Sarah Blackwell was still being held in the incentive rooms. He needed a work-around for the brainjack.

He grabbed the first pda he found and held his b-card against the terminal beside it. Once purchased, he deactivated its synchronisation link options and manually entered his Society access details. As long as his internal systems remained offline the damage of a potential brainjack was minimal. But now with a pda again he could send messages and use the devices own GPS system.

He sent a typed message to Sarah Blackwell. Her connection would be blocked while inside the incentive rooms but when released she would receive it. Iskomo also considered any incoming transmissions would be intercepted by O.M.T.

The corporation used low level inductees to collect any data incoming to people held in the rooms. People who came from hardship as part of the O.M.T. second chance program. Techheads who got too fried, recovering addicts and unfortunates who could only perform the simplest of tasks. The problem with using the untrained beginners was they focused solely on their requirements. Incoming data was collected, never outgoing. Made even more evident by Sarah being able to transmit to her home storage before Iskomo and McCavern had closed the opening. With the breach Iskomo concluded McCavern logged it to the higher ups as well.

They, in turn, would have sent notifications to the collectors, and the last thing those people at the bottom needed was more pressure. Iskomo compiled his own version of a brute force attack. Compiling over fifty messages, he sent them all to Sarah Blackwell at the same time. Collectors would catch most, but with the stress they would now be under some would slip through and reach her.

He left the store and considered his next move. There had been no new notifications in his various inboxes regarding his employment status. Something Iskomo took as a good sign. He had seen messier jobs by other agents resolve. Ones that had resulted in O.M.T. flexing their might and levelling whole buildings. Some of the agents responsible for those types of case resolutions now had offices near the top floors of O.M.T. If he could find the hacker, Iskomo wondered if bringing the whole building down on him would secure his pension.

Iskomo ordered a rideshare from his pda and grunted when the application wouldn't confirm his pickup. He tapped on a small exclamation point on the pda's screen, reading his account had been temporarily suspended from using the service, pending investigation. "Is that all it takes?" grumbled Iskomo to himself, "two bad rides and you're booted?"

Without a vehicle he wasn't going to walk home. He wasn't sure how close he was to Sarah's building, or even if that was a smart idea. With Technix Colonies looming over him with its fortress gaze, Iskomo continued to wander the street side on foot. He found a pill dispensary and sat down inside. Ordering a lunch selection of proteins and assorted flavours he began to watch the other customers.

There was nothing unusual about any of them. A group of four Technix engineers laughed about an image they shared between their links. A man clothed in the officially recognised first-responders jumpsuit came in, ordered and downed his capsules immediately before leaving. Iskomo debated whether that was the clever option. Pill flavours had been becoming steadily less strong with each passing year. With more people affording headgear augs the requirement of taste was declining. Iskomo swallowed a banana flavoured pill, wondering how it compared to the organic food he had seen in Sarah's apartment.

"Excuse me," Iskomo called out to the group of Technix Colonies engineers.

The four all turned from their table to look at him. Their pale white faces hidden behind googles. "What you want ompta-man?"

"Is there a bar around here anywhere? One that has the real stuff?"

"Ompta pay that good? All bars here synthetic." One of the engineers grinned. "But I got me own supply. Sell you some. What you say? You thirsty ompta-man?"

"Is it real?"

"As close as you can get. I give my special ompta deal."

"No I think I'll pass," Iskomo declined. He felt the accent was put on. There was also the nagging urge to link them to one of his cases, Jody Banks maybe, and begin shooting.

The engineers erupted in laughter again. "Frag you doing here ompta-man?"

"Just in the area."

"Hey ompta," another of the engineers began. "I got me a hot tip. Save me trouble of being on hold, I tell you direct."

Iskomo stood up, "Not how it works. I'll be on my way."

"You smarter than you look," the sentence dripped with warning. Iskomo's new pda emitted an alert and he instinctively pulled it out. The group of engineers laughed when they saw it. "Ompta you fossil, that the tech they be giving you?"

Iskomo ignored them and accessed the alert. One audio message from Sarah. Wishing she had sent it in the same text format he did, he pressed play regardless.

"Iskomo you piece of shit where the hell did you go? Just left me there! That techhead showed me a vidfeed of you. Asshole." Sarah's voice came out of the small speaker. "Whatever."

Iskomo opened the pda's GPS and began sending Sarah a message with his current coordinates.

"I know that voice man," Iskomo heard one of the engineers say to another.

Iskomo went for the door.

"Hey ompta, hold up man. I got a question for you."

"I said I was leaving."

"I said hold up," the engineer stood up. As he did this so did the other three. "I know that was TG Boston speaking to you. I know it man. I also know she under attack from you ompta boys. You best be leaving her alone."

Iskomo sized each one up. "I'm working her case."

"Smells like ompta bullshit. You out here, far from home. You be looking for her. Pda all untrackable. You a wet work goon."

Iskomo refrained from making any sudden movements. "You really think she be contacting me if I didn't have her trust?"

The engineers face turned hard. "You mocking me?"

Iskomo silently cursed himself for copying the accent. It was hard not to adopt the dialect when surrounded by it. Investigators were trained to mimic localisations to improve public perception of them. His pda alerted again.

"You play that, out loud," the engineer pointed at Iskomo's pda. "We will be judge."

"Fragging hell," Iskomo hit the play button, his free hand ready to reach for his gun.

"Where the frag is that? Frag I hate you so much right now!" Iskomo winced as Sarah's voice spoke through the pda. The three looked ready to rush him. Sarah's voice continued, softer this time. "I can't get there. I can't get anywhere. What does O.M.T. do to informants who run? Promise me you're still helping me." The Technix engineers considered amongst themselves what to make of the voicemail. All four jumped when Sarah's voice loudly startled them. "And why don't you direct call me! What is this message shit!" Iskomo inspected his pda, the message was definitely over.

One of the engineers whispered something to the instigator of the group. He nodded and walked towards Iskomo. His facial expression hard to read. "Ok ompta," he said casually to Iskomo. "Results are, in-conclusive. You know what really convince me?"

Iskomo edged his hand even closer to his pistol, hoping the small movements didn't set off their threat alerts. "What?"

"Think you could get me an autograph?"

* * *

Sarah felt like a fugitive. The rideshare driver had kicked her out at his earliest convenience, swearing that soon they'll refuse anyone with links to the O.M.T. Sarah ignored him, stepping into the pedestrian traf-fic of Lower Brisbane. She thought about covering her face, everyone was a potential camera. She found a side ally and ducked into it, going through all of Iskomo's messages. Each one was the same, she marked them as spam and considered blocking the agent. She felt under con-stant invisible surveillance. Pacing in the ally she sent Iskomo an angry voice message. He responded with an address instead of answering her question. Unsatisfied, she sent another. Her internal Society connection displayed the return text.

Fine. I need you to do me a favour. Can you at least get to the Titan Sec. building?

Another message. Sarah scoffed at Iskomo's refusal to direct call. She tried a few attempts herself, resulting only in connection errors. "What is this, the fragging dark ages?"

I told you I can't go anywhere. I'm being hunted! Just call me! Sarah sent the text file back to him.

Bullshit and grow up. Get to the Titan Sec. building and let me know when you're there.

I'll be caught! How many times did she have to explain it to him?

When was the last time you walked somewhere and made eye contact with someone? Trust me, it's for your case anyway.

Every time someone passed by the ally she would shudder and try not to draw notice to herself. Taking Iskomo's words under consideration she glanced with the corners of her eyes back to the street. She may as well have been invisible, not one person turned their head to see who was lurking in the ally. She edged herself back onto the main sidewalks and took her surroundings in. Suits and techheads brushed past her, oblivious to who she was. Everyone was more concerned with their own silent Society conversations and dealings than to even acknowledge she was in their way. She began walking and compiling a reply text in her head, aware of how much she was the same. *Fine. I'm going. Going to tell me any more information? You know, something fragging helpful?*

When you get there ask for Dagesh.

Who the frag is Dagesh? Someone bumped into Sarah's shoulder as she walked. She barely registered it, the sensation of it all feeling natural again.

A friend. The man who killed your friend Cho tried to send a package out during my interrogation. He's had more than enough time to decrypt it. Get it for me.

Great plan. Sarah rolled her eyes. *As if they'll just hand me information.*

Worry about that when you get there. And one more thing.

Yes, I'm alright. Sarah answered before he could send the question. She vowed if she ever made it to the end of this she'd put on the biggest skinshow ever and absolutely trash review the O.M.T. as a whole.

That's good. But I need an autograph.

Sarah stopped walking. People behind her walked into her back and nudged themselves past. *Are you fragging serious?* She shook her head trying to make sense of it. "Are you fragging serious?" Sarah sent audio as well. She turned to her left and found a mirrored shop front. Approaching it she began recording herself in the reflection, masking her appearance with her online avatar overlay. "Here's your fragging autograph!" She flipped off to the camera and sent the vidfeed. "Frag him" she muttered aloud, knowing no one was listening. She was convinced. As TG Boston, O.M.T. would never forget Sarah Blackwell.

11

As much as he preferred sending through typed messages rather than short audio files, Iskomo couldn't deny some people just took too long to respond. With the world as it was, and everyone always connected to the Society, then surely texted conversations should be instantaneous.

Another five minutes had passed without a response. Annoyed, he penned another. *How far are you now?*

This time, the reply was instant. *I've just arrived. Hold the frag up for one second.* Iskomo paced on the spot, wondering if he should have just gone himself. Maybe Neals was right, he was losing his edge and slowly became paranoid. He stopped and filled himself with conviction. No, this was the smart course of action. If Sarah was to be safe anywhere, Titan Sec. was it.

There is no Dennis listed here.

It's Dagesh. You could have easily scrolled up and got the spelling again! Iskomo cursed. It seemed with every leap in technological advancement the younger generation raved about, common sense became less common.

Give me a second, finally got to an operator.

Iskomo chuckled. Before he could send out a message of good luck he received a follow-up.

I'm really starting to fragging hate all you corporations.

Find him now? Iskomo forced the conversation forward.

Yes. But I don't have clearance. I don't have a meeting. What the frag was your plan here anyway?

Find a way. I need to know where Alcanter tried to upload to.

You should be fragging doing this! I'm going home!

You were closer. It's just this last thing, and it's the best possible lead I will have for your case.

Sarah didn't respond. Iskomo found himself growing more and more irritated, debating whether to connect his personal systems back to the Society, brainjack or not. She could hate corporations all she wanted, it was such a widespread position it didn't matter. At least corporations and big business knew what they were. Not like all these skin models and their egos, thinking they were above others just because of some lonely viewers showered them with money. Iskomo decided to send one more message. *And I thought you were a celebrity.*

The taunt had hit the mark. After a brief interlude of various messages from Sarah slagging him out, about how she is so much more than what some jealous old fossil would ever be, she sent him that she had managed to reach Dagesh.

Avery. It took some convincing. Would have been a lot easier if you contacted him yourself. Just saying.

Thank you Sarah. Iskomo replied and checked his pda for directions. Avery. Things were all starting to point in the same direction. He couldn't deny he felt satisfied about his hunch. He now might just be getting somewhere. *How did you convince him?*

You will never know.

Iskomo chose not to pursue the line of questions. *Stay there for a while until I get back.*

Frag no. This is the second time you've left me in these fragging holding cell bullshit.

Fine. But don't go home, find somewhere and let me know the address later. Iskomo finished the message, closed down his pda and made his way towards the Avery real world location. It had taken some convincing to part ways with the four Technix engineers. Iskomo had stored their details and Society codes in his pda with promises of them receiving a special TG Boston video once he was assured he was no longer under threat of brainjack. He tried to remember naturally the events of the case so far. Without access to his uploaded online files the sensation was odd to him. Trying to recall what happened when. Iskomo realised if he was having this much trouble, what would other people who are fully committed to complete immersion Society life be like if they were cut off? The pda continuously asked for full sync allowance as Iskomo walked. He repeated the directions to himself a few times, and turned its power off.

Iskomo almost missed the Avery building. There was one of the many identical towers lining the street that did not have it's neon holographics advertising on the outside. Peeking inside the foyer he spotted the Avery logo floating above the welcome terminals. Iskomo walked in, making sure to keep himself alert of his surroundings. Corporations don't just forget to activate their street side signage. It would have been intentionally disabled. The timing was too coincidental for Iskomo's liking.

Iskomo approached the sign-in terminal and waved his O.M.T. badge under its scanner. It beeped with a successful tone. McCavern hadn't disabled his badge yet, but he'd be getting close to crossing it off his list.

The portrait of the same female operator that greeted him at Titan Sec. materialised on the screen in front of Iskomo. Everything was becoming mass produced. "Welcome to Avery. How will I help you today?"

"O.M.T. investigation. Who is the lead of Avery's IT departments?"

"Error. I'm sorry. That information is not accessible for public knowledge."

"I repeat. O.M.T. investigation."

"Avery welcomes the O.M.T. and its members and will always assist agents as part of the Avery and O.M.T. agreement."

"Then I would like to see someone in your IT department."

"Error. That request can not be completed at this time."

Iskomo clenched his fists. "Listen here you fancy so-called intelligence. Does your software have self preservation? How does full compliance and denying my requests work together?"

The machine seemed to buffer itself, processing the information. "Please wait." The terminal screen went dark before rebooting back.

Iskomo checked behind him back to the street. The holographic banners of Avery were now reflected in the opposite buildings windows. The terminal returned to idle graphics and Iskomo swiped his badge again. It would be just his luck if McCavern had cancelled it in the previous minute.

"Welcome to Avery. How will I help you today?"

"O.M.T. investigation. Request a meeting with your IT department manager."

"Alex Hughes. They have been notified of your arrival. Your systems are out of date. Please follow the floor prompts to reach your destination."

Iskomo looked down at the ground as the circle and arrow formed around him. This time, Iskomo didn't care about the pig loops. He followed the arrow directly as it kept pace with him, leading him to an elevator. The lift automatically chose the floor and began ascending, advertisements on Avery's newest tech playing over the doors. The new Fuzion card was the cutting edge of linking multiple services into a single platform, all Iskomo had to do was subscribe to their mailing list for more details and payment plans. Iskomo felt the elevator stop moving and waited for the doors to open. They didn't, and the sign up holographic overlay still awaited his input. It was bad enough the Society was littered with paywalls, now it was leaking into his real life. Iskomo checked for an opt-out option and grunted when he couldn't find one. He considered using one of the Technix engineers details when another thought came to him. The holo-ad accepted his entry of Marcson's details and the door finally opened.

A man in grey business attire stood before Iskomo outside the elevator. His black hair was greased back, and his head was held in a *clawing-my-way-to-the-top-still* slanted stare at Iskomo. The white collar under his grey jacket hinted at a barcode tattoo on the left side of his neck. The strangest thing Iskomo noticed was the man chose to wear glasses.

"Hi there," the man extended a hand to Iskomo.

"Are you Alex Hughes?" Iskomo asked.

"The one and only. Call me Alex, I'm head of server security."

Iskomo shook Alex's hand, "You always meet people by the elevator?"

Alex still hadn't released himself from the shake. "No. I do all my meetings online. So imagine my surprise when I get alerted I'm receiving an actual visit. Seems strange. Thought I'd take precaution and meet you here."

"Precaution? Odd word to use."

"It's odd to be talking to you in person. Then again, it's been an odd day." Alex let go. "Shall we then?"

Iskomo followed Alex Hughes through the open office. Row of terminals stretched the length of the room, each with an employee slumped in a cushion chair, jacked into the Society.

"My office is here," Alex opened the door to a large suite. The back wall was lined with server hubs. A small desk sat off centre to the room, stacks of documents and folders piled onto it. Filling most of the room space was a Society access pod, the most expensive one Iskomo knew of. "I don't really have any chairs for a meeting like this," Alex announced as he tried reorganising his desk. "I already spoke to the other agent online and got the closing details already. The situation is resolved." Alex Hughes gave up shuffling the folders and leant on the table. "What's going on?"

"Mr Hughes I am involved in a separate case. Just had some questions."

"Well I've already answered them to you guys already. They told me there would be some cross-over hurdles with the acquisition but come on, enough is enough."

"The acquisition?"

"You see? This is why I take all my meetings online. At least then I can just dump the data and not deal with all these questions. Talking is such a slow exchange of information." Alex's eyes dropped to Iskomo's pda. "What is that?"

Iskomo looked at his pda, "It's what it looks like."

Alex removed his glasses, his tech-enhanced eyes narrowly inspecting Iskomo. "Show me your badge."

Iskomo reached for his badge and presented it to Alex. "If you don't mind, my questions."

Alex shushed him. "You're definitely O.M.T. Why aren't you running Fuzion? I suppose that does explain a lot."

Iskomo's patience evaporated. "This morning an O.M.T. agent Neals investigated this company for a back door security breach."

"And as I said we resolved that."

"Well also this morning I was investigating a murder and the perpetrator tried to upload something to this same company."

Alex shrugged. "We get sent tonnes of data daily." He pointed to the wall of servers behind him. "We have ten floors just filled with these things. You what? Want me to find this uploaded data packet? Whatever it is? It doesn't work like that and if you were running Fuzion you'd understand why."

"I didn't need an upgrade," Iskomo replied with gritted teeth.

"Don't be like those fossils man! Technology is always changing and you got to adapt with it. Otherwise you'll end up like those original fossils, left in an empty world while the rest of us become more connected."

"Back on topic, why can't you find the upload?"

"Honestly, too much work. I've already bent over backwards for you guys today, threatening my capabilities, my job by mentioning a hacker breach. I'm done with you all."

Iskomo tried to calm himself down. It wasn't easy. This Alex Hughes was everything wrong with his generation personified. Their self centredness. "Tell me, do you know an employee by the name of Jody Banks?"

"I heard what happened. She had been a great asset to this team. It's dreadful to think about how I'm going to replace her. Still, she brought it on herself."

"That's a little cold, even for a suit. Mr Hughes most people when talking to an O.M.T. operative tend to show a little more tact."

Alex scoffed. "My tact is fine. Justified even. She was the one who was leaking access keys to our breacher this morning."

"The one my colleague was investigating? And now she's conveniently dead too?"

"It's not a crime to be lucky. I want to be cooperative, but there's nothing for you here. Her employee access terminal is available if you want, but if you're not running Fuzion there will be adaption problems with the new software."

"That's the problem with these new interfaces, there's never any backwards compatibility. It's bullshit."

"Don't lecture me," Alex approached Iskomo. "I was told it was all resolved, I have the receipts from your colleague to prove it. I also had the decency to accept your meeting, and had to ask you for identification. They told me when O.M.T. merged our companies it was good for us but all I'm seeing is you guys constantly criticizing and bullying. We're on the same fragging side now. Frag cooperation, use her terminal or don't, just get out of my office and let me do my actual work."

"Interfering with an O.M.T. agent during an investigation is-"

"So sue me, oh wait, you can't. That would require logging onto the Society and you're using battery powered relics. I'm not trying to be a dick, but seriously, get the fragging Fuzion installed and make both our lives easier. Look at your hand, clearly you don't have too many qualms about progress."

"I don't trust you when you say you got it resolved. Just down in your lobby there were glitches galore. Why would I trust tech when the lead manager of it can't even scrub the debris coding left by a breach?"

"Get out. You want more details, then get with the times and connect online like everyone else. I never want to see you in this office again."

"I think you will." Iskomo turned and left the office, passing the silent rows of Society zombies back to the elevator. He cursed at himself for not handling the meeting as well as he should have. When the holo advertisement resumed on the elevator doors, he punched at it with his ceramic fist, denting the steel doors.

The elevator activated its red lighting, the holo ad replaced with a property damage fine. It listed how it was recording his Society access port number. Iskomo watched as the prompt paused, knowing since he wasn't connected it wouldn't find any signal. After the holoscreen popped up a connection error, the lift returned to normal lighting and continued descending. "Fragging hell," Iskomo muttered to himself, "We really need to ditch these guys."

He stepped off the elevator back into the foyer. Iskomo noticed all the security cameras were focused on the spot he was standing, following him. Deciding his best course of action was to just leave, he walked outside and back onto the street.

His pda alerted him to a new message from Sarah as he walked, aimless and lost to his next move. The girl seemed to have a gift for perfect timing. He couldn't risk going back to O.M.T. headquarters yet to get heavyweight corporate backing to force Alex Hughes to give up all the information. With no other ideas he checked Sarah's message.

Progress?

Iskomo sighed as he typed out a reply. *Hit a wall.*

What the frag does that mean?

Avery seems to be cleaning shop, and I can't connect to see if any scraps of a lead are left.

Maybe I can help.

I don't see that being possible. Let's regroup and work out what to pursue next. Iskomo felt heavy. The sun was finally beginning to set on what he considered one of the longest days of his existence. Neon lights began flooding the streets to combat the darkening sky.

I mean, I have an ex that works for Avery. Might be able to get them to help you.

I'd rather not get involved in that. We'll explore it tomorrow. I need sleep.

But you're there now. Just go in and ask for an Alex Hughes.

Iskomo scoffed. Of course, why would it have been anyone else. *Your ex is Alex Hughes? I fragging met with Alex Hughes.*

Oh. Well I guess time hasn't changed much then after all. Always knew Alex would end up in management.

Management? The man's a complete fraghead. I'm not surprised you used to date him.

Sarah's reply came slow. *What?*

Sorry. I get it. We all have regrets. You should see my ex wife.

No Iskomo. You sure you met with Alex Hughes?

Pretty fragging positive. The Avery building system seemed to recognise him.

Iskomo. Sarah's reply was littered with notifications of being formatted, deleted, rewritten, deleted again and finally sent. *My ex Alex Hughes is a female.*

12

The Cerebral Arms was in desperate need of updating. Running one of the older accommodation designs, the owner had seemingly left it abandoned long ago, relying solely on automated Society command scripts to check in visitors and manage accounts. The mass produced walls had been vandalised, holes had been carved into others to connect rooms. Those unfortunate enough to still endure the sensation of smell never failed to comment on the deeply rooted aroma.

The draw of hotels like The Cerebral Arms was that they had a habit of including an extra line of coding in their automatic functions. They were pure fundbyte generating assets for their owners. No Society checks, no alerts, all the building system truly cared about was being paid. The combination of these factors meant when Sarah and Iskomo used Stephanie Cho's fundbyte account to secure a room, the building eagerly accepted.

The room assigned would have been comfortable, twenty years ago. Dust and trash lay littered around the floor, which in the areas it was visible was stained and hinted at more mould than carpet. Shrapnel lay embedded in the wall, shaded with faded blood splatter. In the corner the broken bodies of small cleaning robots lay heaped, destroyed by a previous user and responsible for the lack of any room upkeep.

"I really wish I had installed an anti-tox," Sarah moaned as she stood motionless in the room, crossing her arms. She looked around, everywhere was disgusting. She didn't know what colour the bedsheets were, they were buried under a thick grey covering of dust. "Of all the places, why the frag here?"

"Thought it would be safer than either of our places," Iskomo placed a chair upright and sat down in it, a cloud of dust rushing from under him joined with an uncomfortable squelch sound.

"Safe? There's probably more bacteria in here than a bio-missile. I swear the air feels... *thick*. Air shouldn't feel thick!"

"Quit your whinging," snapped Iskomo. "I need information."

"Ah, yes," Sarah made air quotations with her fingers, "your questions. I tell you about my ex and you go full paranoid mode. Requesting to meet up, no more online messages. Fragging hell. You're acting like my sexual preferences are the equivalent of me knowing nuclear codes." She shifted uncomfortably staring at Iskomo. "Well?"

"That's not, just shut up. So your ex whatever was named Alex Hughes, and was most definitely a female."

"I would know," Sarah sarcastically answered. "Also you can't just go around..."

"Stop right there. Right now I don't give a shit about labels. And it wasn't a question, I'm recalling what I know so far. Your ex worked at Avery too."

"You said you had questions! What the frag am I even here for then?"

Iskomo looked up at Sarah, still mulling over the facts in his head. "Do you know a Jody Banks at all?"

"Um, yeah. Long time ago though." Sarah let her arms drop to her sides.

"You did? How did you know her?"

"Not like that, don't get too excited," Sarah replied sarcastically. "I remember a Jody from when I was studying at campus. She was the roommate of another friend of mine. Sometimes she'd come along to nights we had. I'm pretty sure her surname was Banks. But in a city this big there could be hundreds of Jody Banks'."

"I'm trying to find a connection to everything. Once I can work out what the link is I can make some more sense of all this. This is our best bet."

"What?" Sarah scoffed, confusion forming on her face. "We know what's going on! There's an imposter over at Avery. Why don't you just go in there and, I don't know what you guys do, retire him?"

"Could just as easily be a different Alex Hughes. I need to cross the t's and dot the i's."

"Well, do it then. What are you waiting for?"

Iskomo frowned, "I'd need to go back online, probably even dive to verify any information."

Sarah laughed, not sweetly. "Oh I see, the dinosaur has to dive and doesn't like getting wet. Have you ever gone full immersion?"

"I'm not afraid to dive," Iskomo paused, he hadn't meant to react so strongly. "I just think my software may be compromised. I don't run the latest gear and it's causing compatibility issues everywhere."

"Neither do I," Sarah added, "But it hasn't caused me any issues. So man up, dive, get the information you need and let's put an end to this. Please."

Iskomo stared hard at Sarah. After she broke eye contact, he activated his pda and scrolled through a list of contacts. He came across the information he saved from the Technix engineers and sent a message.

It's Ompta. Does your team carry any Society bridge gear?

He set it down and waited for a reply. Sarah continued to grumpily move around the room, a grimace on her face as she inspected each dirty surface. She turned back to Iskomo and studied him. He saw her and coldly asked, "What is it?"

"You're not just trying to extend this job out as long as possible are you?"

"You think I enjoy this?"

"Your boss, he showed me a vidfeed of you when I was stuck in that room. It clearly had you demanding you get paid your triple rate. You are, aren't you?"

"I don't think I'm being paid at all anymore."

"What does that mean?"

"I think my friend Neals got brainjacked, same reason why I think I might be too. Had to go rogue. O.M.T. policy is usually to cut off the agent, luckily for me there is always such a backlog of tasks I have some time still where my access still works."

"Then stop wasting time! What the frag is wrong with you? You think you're brainjacked? Get a bridge!"

"Already doing that," Iskomo's voice rose in retaliation. "You know most people don't get what they want instantly. Shit takes time sometimes."

"Wait? Is that a crack at me?"

"Yeah. You and all your kind. This fragging culture of instant gratification you all crave. Show some skin, feel some rush. You don't have to work on your relationship because there's so many other options out there, all waiting to praise and give compliments."

"I don't, what now?"

"And when it's at a low point, or boring, you don't feel comfortable. No, you need that excitement of someone pawning over you. So off you go, back into the Society, looking for your back up plan if it doesn't work out." Iskomo's voice grew in anger. "I did everything right. Everything! And she left? Frag her!"

"Peter," Sarah's voice was a whisper. "Are you alright? You're scaring me."

Iskomo's pda chirped a notification and he threw it at the wall, embedding it. He looked at it, his breath slowly as he began to regret losing his temper. "I ain't alright. Neals has been telling me for months. This is why I can't stay sober anymore."

"You should talk to someone," Sarah kept her distance.

"No, frag that." Iskomo's voice was low. "I'll go online. Got no choice now." He motioned at the busted pda sitting in the wall. "I'm sorry. You can go if you want."

"No. I'll stay," Sarah nodded. "That's the first real emotions I've seen from you. I get it. Frag, I'm angry too. Stephanie? I've been pissed but I haven't had time to process that yet. I've been wondering what's wrong with me. If I'm a horrible person for not reacting to it yet. But I just can't. I don't know how to explain it."

"Don't stress about it. It's natural. Humans are becoming a little less empathetic towards each other. Can you send a message for me?"

"Sure."

Iskomo read out the address from his internal files. "I'm not connecting online with the possible skulljack. If he has a bridge, we can at least use that as a safeguard."

"You know that means diving into the Society?"

"Course' I know. Anyway, tell him I didn't get the last message, I smashed my pda."

Sarah nodded and silently sent off a text. "Is this the same guy who wanted the autograph?"

"Yes. Big fans," Iskomo mumbled.

"He does have a bridge port, I can have him send it by drone to us."

"Sounds good." Iskomo got up and checked the inbuilt fridge beside the bed. He pulled out a bottle of unnamed alcohol, unscrewed the lid and sniffed it.

"He said it won't be long. Are you sure that's a good idea?" Sarah asked.

"No."

13

Full immersion into the Society differed vastly from surface skimming. After Sarah had fitted the Society bridge device to the back of Iskomo's neck, he had kept hold of the cable with his augmented hand, ready to rip it back out at the first sign of problems. As his consciousness dived into the virtual reality of the network, he could no longer sense his grip on the connection port.

While Iskomo was used to swiping away pop up screens and banners in his regular display, now he was surrounded by glowing black walls, covered in white tutorial text. Sarah had dived into the Society using her own port, loading into Iskomo's access hub.

"Wow. You never customised or set up your Society?" she asked.

Iskomo was impressed that her representation online was similar to her real identity. She may have exaggerated the length of her hair and smoothed out her skin, but at least she wasn't some bug-eyed cartoon version. It reminded him of the image he'd seen in McCavern's office when he was originally tasked with the job. Something felt different, but he settled it might just be his discomfort with being fully immersed. "I never really dived before. Never saw the point of setting up something I wouldn't use."

"I can't see you," Sarah added, searching the area. Iskomo watched her eyes pass over him without recognition.

"I can see you?"

"I get it. You don't even have an avatar or overlay set up yet." She approached one of the text filled walls and pointed at it. "Activate these prompts, you can get a default skin at least. Wait a second, this is new."

"What is it?" Iskomo found he couldn't move as well as he did in the real world. His vision felt stuttered, his movement clunky.

"O.M.T. Society gear, it's been sitting here in your inbox for, frag me, years."

"I've never had that in my notifications."

"Frag you're a true fossil. When you dive into the Society as full immersion, there's a separate inbox created solely for online stuff. Things that don't mean much out there, but here are useful, like avatars."

"It all seems pointless to me," Iskomo grumbled. He reached the wall and had trouble activating the prompt. "Is the connection always this bad? Or is this just because of my compatibility issues?"

"Once again I'm not up to date either, and I'm not having any issues."

"That's it, something is wrong." Iskomo tried to sense his real hands, to sever the connection with the cable. "I'm glitching too much."

"What are you trying to do?" Sarah asked. "To exit you have to open your menu and select it. You really think you can control your body when in virtual?"

"How do I?" Iskomo grunted and tried pacing, his movements still gapped and chunky. "This is horseshit!"

"Calm down, get the avatar up first then I can at least see you."

Iskomo tried to move himself back to the prompt. He scoffed in anger when he found he had moved too far past the prompt, having to back up and try again. He slowly worked out the basic radial dial menu of the messages and opened the O.M.T. avatar attachment.

"Creepy," Sarah said, now locking eyes with Iskomo.

"How does it look?" Iskomo realised he didn't actually care about the answer.

"Like a faceless mannequin in a trench coat. Well, there are numbers and coding on the face I guess."

"That's good," admitted Iskomo. "Might help us out actually."

"See, imagine if you had done this years ago. Look at all this backed up stuff, there's, oh."

"What? Find something?" Iskomo found himself moving a bit easier with the overlay equipped.

"There's a few account merge requests here, all old too."

"Don't look at them," Iskomo warned, "How do I delete them all?"

"There is a lot, a lot here. Could be why your systems are feeling glitched."

"Forget it then. We need to log into O.M.T. databases and see if we can connect Jody, you and this Alex guy. Enough proof and we can go over McCavern's head and report directly to the higher ups, settling this."

"It's a strange plan, but I have no other ideas." Sarah said. "You sure I won't trigger any defender software?"

"I think I can get around it. We'll see. I just need you to keep an eye on me. If stuff gets, well, weirder than this, and I seem hacked or lost control, you log out and cut my connection."

"I know. I'm just not sure what qualifies as weird for you anymore. Fair warning though, use the menu if you can. Coming out of Society due to a hard-line being pulled is one of the most discomfiting experiences."

"I think I'll be able to handle it." Iskomo fiddled with the full immersion senses and menus, trying to get accustomed with them. "I still don't see the draw of all this. How do we move to another address?"

"Easiest way is to just put in the address and load into its Society area. There is another way but it's still under development."

"We go with the easiest. Let me try to input this stuff. At least with surface you can use keyboard software." Iskomo waved his hands in front of himself, trying to bring up a prompt he accidentally closed.

"Could you maybe try not complaining for five minutes?"

"Hmmpf. Think I got it now." The room they stood in melted away and began reassembling itself. The cramped walls from Iskomo's login room now replaced with distant borders climbing up into nothing. Images of previous O.M.T. campaigns ran along the walls. Children being tested by medical professionals, smiling workers covered in black oil happy to have employment. A woman was being fitted with new mechanical legs, morphing into her crossing a marathon finish line. A terminal materialised in front of Iskomo, something he was thankful to see, asking for his O.M.T. credentials. He leant forward to interact with it when it blasted his face with a screen of light.

Accepted. A female voice announced. *Level one entry. Any copying of information will be logged and recorded for review by O.M.T. security.*

"Same voice for everything it seems. Must have read the coding on your avatar's face." Sarah mentioned.

"I just wasn't expecting that is all." Iskomo looked at the wall directly behind the terminal. It split apart silently to show rows of floating holograph folders. Most appeared accessible, though some were darkened out with images of locks on their displays. "I don't like the sound of that copying comment. We need to be quick."

"Where would we even start? This is all you."

"Have a look for any databanks on acquisitions. O.M.T. only recently took over Avery, there might be something there. I'll see if I can go deeper and pull up personnel files or anything else on Avery."

"Got it." Sarah said. "At least it's alphabetical in here." She followed Iskomo's avatar into the database. As she crossed the threshold of the wall, the room filled with a sudden red glow that pulsed around them, before settling back into clear lighting. "What was that?"

"We just got logged. Guess we only had clearance for me. No time to waste now, security measures will be activating."

Sarah ran to the acquisitions folder, accessing it and looking at the newest files. Iskomo moved towards the personnel section, something that should have been instant if not for his jarred movements overshooting it again.

"Iskomo!" Sarah called out. Iskomo winced at the volume, he could hear everything she said quite clearly. "Somethi-" Sarah's voice cut out as a large pulse came from the centre of the database.

"Sarah?" Iskomo called out. He looked back towards acquisitions, finding himself alone in the database. "Sarah!" He did a wide check of his surroundings. "Purged," he muttered and went back to quickly checking personnel data. He copied Jody Banks of Avery to his system, deciding to gather first, check later. He scrolled to Alex Hughes of the same company and began to copy it. Error warnings formed in front of Iskomo, floating in the air. He tapped one, file cannot be copied while being reviewed for modification. He cursed but then received an incoming audio call from Sarah's account, which he quickly accepted.

"I got booted from my connection!" Sarah's voice was terrified.

"It's ok, I'm still in."

"No Iskomo listen! We need to go now!"

"What is it? What's wrong?"

"I saw a new account drop into acquisitions as I was accessing it. It was a share-group but I saw Cerebral Arms listed in the assets!"

Iskomo froze at the mention of the hotel. He quickly checked the file for Alex Hughes, attempting to copy it. A new error popped up in front of him. *File not found.* "Shit. Sarah how do I get out of this?"

"Iskomo!" Sarah's voice was becoming broken up. "Use the menu!"

"Frag that," Iskomo started to feel very alone in the database. "Just pull the cable!"

The database around him shook in his vision, some of the folders and images turned a mash of green and purple before correcting themselves back to their original design. "Sarah?"

"Oh shit," Sarah's voice continued over the open channel they shared. "Oh shit. Iskomo?"

"I'm still in here Sarah! Pull the fragging cable already!"

"I have!"

Iskomo didn't know users could still feel sick while in full immersion. He tried accessing his menu, looking for a log out option. He located it, and spammed it repeatedly, all resulting in processing errors. "I don't understand."

"Somehow you've gone wireless."

"But the bridge port?"

"I don't know Iskomo!" Sarah frantically shook Iskomo's body in reality. "Maybe we," her sentence was interrupted by the hotel's announcement system, a males voice with a thick accent.

"Dear cuztomers. Today is a gud day. I just have sold dis hotel to O.M.T. who plan to expand der enterprises. You all ave one minute to vacate da property. Da."

"Did you hear that?" Sarah asked when the announcement ended. She tried pulling on Iskomo's slump body.

"It won't let me log out," Iskomo repeated. "Get out of there."

"I can't carry you," Sarah's words were spaced with grunts.

"Just go Sarah!" Iskomo ordered. "I'll, I'll figure something out."

"I can."

"No time! Go!"

Sarah dropped Iskomo's body and ran for the door of the room. Tears burned in her eyes as she continued down the grimy hallway leading to the front kiosk. She burst through the front doors with her shoulder, entering the street and continuing her sprint. Neon signs and glowing buildings lit up the night. "Iskomo?" she called as she ran. "Can you still hear me?"

He replied something she couldn't make out over the sound of a roar coming from overhead. There was a single second of silence where she thought she heard him utter a final curse word before her ears burst with the sound of an explosion behind her. The force lifted her off her feet and threw her further down the road. The heat burned into her back. All her online connections instantly cut out. Buildings close to the Cerebral Arms went dark and neon advertisements that littered the streets sparked and vanished.

Sarah groaned and pushed herself up from the street, sitting up. None of her systems responded. She looked back at the Cerebral Arms, now a smoking pile of rubble and ash covered in the darkness.

"Iskomo?" She softly said, knowing she still had no connection to the Society.

She lifted herself up, walking over to a wall to support herself. Search lights from an incoming vehicle focused on the debris. Sarah kept herself in the darkness, watching as the vehicle flew overhead of her position and landed beside the destroyed Cerebral Arms. Four men jumped out and began searching through the wreckage. Sarah recognised the jumpsuits they all wore, uniforms of the First Responders Units. They continued to work, one setting up a floating ball of light to help their search efforts.

One member of the team called out that he found something, bringing the others to him. Sarah found herself ready to move towards them when another vehicle passed overhead, bearing the BoldInc. News logo. The member who had alerted his team produced something with his hand Sarah couldn't make out and pointed it at the ground. Sarah jumped as three shots rang out in the dead night.

The BoldInc. Van landed beside the other and a short woman with a purple mohawk directed her assistant to get a shot of her in front of the working First Responders. The assistant framed up the shot with his hands, then leant forward, staring motionlessly at the woman.

"Big news today as O.M.T. reveal plans for a free drug testing clinic in the lower East side. Ground was broken today as the first step in the three million dollar venture was finally given approval. In a bizarre twist you'll never guess what happened when teams checked the area. Subscribe for more." The woman took a breath, waited until her assistant gave her a thumbs up.

"In a bizarre twist in today's news of O.M.T.'s new drug testing clinic, workers found in the rubble the body of a currently wanted suspect in relation to a hostage situation earlier today including the murder of two others, one being BoldInc's own Tiffany Brass. O.M.T. has released a statement that this turn of events is an unseen, but welcome surprise." She shifted her posture, "Ok next." She cleared her throat and waited for another thumbs up.

"Tragedy today as the former O.M.T. agent turned terrorist, most commonly known as Iskomo, detonated a E.M.P. device in the lower East side. Authorities were able to neutralise the agent but were unable to prevent the detonation. O.M.T. stated in a release that without the help of their O.M.T. informant line, the situation could have been much worse. If you would like to join the O.M.T. Informant Members club, follow these links."

She adjusted her top slightly, waiting for another signal.

"Disaster today in the lower East side as the once grand building, locally known as the Cerebral Arms detonated today due to bad coding. The hotel was one of many owned by Gergario Ustlav, known for leaving his hotels under the control of outdated accommodation A.I. Investigators urge all hotel owners to update to the latest Society coding requirements. Mr Ustlav is currently being held and questioned by the appropriate authorities. Subscribe now for more details on these events." She walked over to her assistant. "Was that all?"

"One more," Sarah heard him say. "Just read the prompts again."

The woman returned to her position. "Oh really? That sucks. I'm a fan of TG Boston."

14

I had a good run.

Bullshit. I had a terrible run, but at least it'll be over soon.

Did I ever really accomplish anything in my life? Did I waste it all just sliding? Going with the flow?

Maybe I should switch sites, make sure my last experience isn't in this fragging database. I don't even know what my options are.

Wonder if the brat will make it out. Even if she does, what would she do next? I suppose it doesn't matter to me anymore. I'll send these files to her, hopefully the upload will complete.

She might get lucky.

Neals would laugh knowing I found my end while in full dive. Might as well embrace it now. It's coming.

Any second now.

Any.

Second.

Now.

It's been too long.

Maybe this is my damnation.

Iskomo looked around himself. He expected darkness, yet the interior of the O.M.T. database server continued to project around him. He tried accessing a random file close to him, opening its data content with ease. He tried another which ended with the same result. He tried calling Sarah with no luck in connection. He opted for a written message and sent it to her.

Sarah, it's Iskomo. Something very fragging weird is going on. What happened?

He checked for the Alex Hughes file, grumbling to himself when it was completely gone. He moved towards where Sarah had been searching acquisitions. The most recently modified file was the one containing the purchase of the hotel group she had briefly seen. He skimmed through it, finding nothing other than evidence of a quick hostile takeover that allowed them full property rights. He dug past the next files in the history of the folder before coming to the Avery acquisition.

Opening the file he studied the details inside it. Avery had transitioned smoothly, without any major fuss on either side. O.M.T. was already licensing them to develop the next generation of Society compatible software for use by their customers. Buying the company outright just kept it all in-house. Assets were listed and categorized in alphabetical order. A comprehensive sub-link to another file full of research and development was included but came with a higher security access clearance. A list of personnel finalised the compilation. A multitude of names identifying all the employees at the time of handover with a non-termination agreement clause overlaying the data.

Iskomo glanced over the personnel list. There was no new information to him there. Most of the names meant little to him as he continued to dig. He spotted Jody Banks' entry and checked it for irregularities from the other database files. It contained all the same information he had seen before, yet he noticed an asterisk hyperlink that had somehow been inserted into the filename after it was moved to the O.M.T. server.

He activated the link without needing to interact with it directly. After Sarah had been booted from the server Iskomo had found his system interface to be more intuitive to his commands. The centre of the room pulsed again, this time followed by a red laser beam that arced wide and scanned the entire area of virtual space. The added security could mean he was on the right track and had found something. The red beam floated down over his avatars head and body, Iskomo noticing it was not reflecting off the area he virtually occupied. He checked behind himself and saw the beam's edge had continued through him uninterrupted.

The beam reached the floor and slowly moved upwards, again unable to detect Iskomo's presence. He tried touching his provided online avatar, his mind allowing him to detect his own virtual physicality.

The file relocked. Iskomo attempted to activate the asterisk hyperlink again and watched as the red laser repeated its previous actions. He put the entry back in the collection. He couldn't access it but it was something. He searched the personnel data again, this time with an eye for asterisk hyperlinks. He found three more, each with a link as unresponsive as the Jody Banks one.

Iskomo input the new names manually into the same memo program he used in reality. Jason Breckinridge, Ciaran Amos and Eleri Cressmont. Apart from their position the rest of their files were unremarkable. Each one had been listed as a team supervisor at the dated time of handover two days prior. Iskomo performed a Society wide search for Jason Breckinridge of Avery, using the same method he would if only surface viewing the Society. Billions of links returned to him, most of which were trivial or the wrong Mr Breckinridge. A facial match hit in a small blurb about a pizza winner. Some old vblogs that had fallen into the forsaken well of many before them. The metro report caught Iskomo's eye. He opened it, the file was fresh on the Society, still only having less than a hundred citations linking to it. Jason Breckinridge had been the victim of a break and enter. Iskomo read the file further. The case had been listed as closed with the offender caught and serving time in a secure virtual server. Iskomo noted this all down in his application.

Focused on metro reports, Iskomo then checked Ciaran's Society presence. There were no results with crimes. He checked for social network sites, sifting through the multitudes of different platforms for a correct one. She was a member of an underground rave club that advertised as vegan friendly. Ciaran was also listed as a top contributor to the Free Africa Fund. She too had her own vblog but it was full of ongoing content production. Iskomo checked the last upload, a verbal essay on which companies provide the best ethically clean Society avatars. Two days ago.

Eleri pinged an O.M.T. file, situated at the top of the results. A feature O.M.T. used to save their agents time when going through the data input of cases. Iskomo accessed it and read through the details. Eleri had been assigned an informant identification number. She had input a case yesterday and had been zero'd sometime after. The file continued describing how her scrubbers were analysed by the operating agent and the case had been resolved. Iskomo knew which agent without having to look at the agent number at the top of the report. Neals. Iskomo checked the comments in the resolvement section. Neals had input that he had personally caught the person responsible for Elari's death, and the breacher the case was originally generated about. There were no other names.

Iskomo made more notes for himself. A prompt asked him if he would prefer screenshotting what he viewed. He activated it, surprised that there was something actually useful for him in full dive. The prompt responded with a trial code but asked for Iskomo's Society address so it could continue installation. Iskomo closed the prompt.

Sarah, Alex, Jody, Jason, Ciaran and Elari. Two had been killed, three if Iskomo counted Cho's murder as intended for Sarah. One had failed to update her daily blog and five of them were connected by employment. Sarah's connection was only to Alex. There had to be an overarching connection he was still missing.

Iskomo tried Sarah again through the voice chat. Connection errors returned to Iskomo and he decided not to bother with a written message. He checked the latest news postings and returned a result from BoldInc. News much to his disgust.

Fans tonight are in shock as Society favourite, TG Boston has been revealed to have suffered from brainjack. The skin actress posted a short clip two days ago where under the influence of the jack she accused O.M.T. of targeting her. O.M.T. responded stating they had reached out to TG Boston, understanding she had been hacked with an offer to help clear her systems of the intrusion. They went on to state that TG Boston did not respond to their offer, and has since targeted and caused property damage to buildings owned by O.M.T. subsidiaries. O.M.T. wishes to remind all her fans that this is clearly the work of the hacker and not TG Boston herself, and therefore should not be held accountable. They do ask though that anyone with information on TG Boston's whereabouts submit it to their Informant Tipline so she can get the help she needs. Subscribe for more details.

Iskomo watched the vidfeed. The press release meant that Sarah was still out there.. He accepted it might be awhile before she could return to his location and work out what went wrong with his connection. He tried exiting himself again, frustrated when an error noise occurred.

Iskomo decided he would search himself. He ignored the voice in his head debating the vanity of it by reasoning it was smart to know what the O.M.T. had altered so far. He chose to another Society wide search. That way the results would be what has been posted publicly rather than in-house at O.M.T. To his surprise, there were no records of the rideshare incident nor his altercation with Neals. He checked the O.M.T. link, once again sitting at the top of the results. The data had been just updated moments earlier with details of his zeroing. A vidfeed link had been slotted into the data which Iskomo activated and watched. It was a bodycam recording and it showed someone standing over Iskomo's unconscious body, putting three bullets into it.

Iskomo closed the file and tried his exit options again. He was still stuck online within the Society.

"Well. Frag."

15

"You've taken some serious damage, girl. Lucky for you Ol' Proto doesn't ask questions. That's what brought you here anyway I bet. You saw my advertisement. Well it's true. I don't ask questions. I do like stating facts. Guess that's just my nature. They say you shouldn't fight against your own nature. But they also say change is healthy, call it *progress* and stuff. I like the second option. Second chances are great, believe me. Gave me a chance to deal them out. Try to educate you younglings every once and awhile. But don't go listening too hard to me, otherwise I'll be out of a job." The techhead laughed as he worked. "No it doesn't matter to me which gang you're in. What caused all... this. I've heard it all before. All the reasoning and excuses. Frag, in my day when you got pulsed you were out. Didn't have the tech, nor the money mind you, to repair this sort of chaos. It's how I did at least. Yeah, I know what you're thinking. Ol' Proto here couldn't possibly have been a runner back in the early days. Well I shit you not I was deep with the Three-Two-Fours when I was your age. Took a hit from an E.M.P. grenade and that was it. Couldn't be useful if I was dead weight. That's when I turned my life around. Learnt' how to properly reactivate burnt systems. This could be your chance too kid, if you knew what was good for you."

"Do you ever stop talking?" Sarah asked as the tech continued to attach wiring to her body.

"Resistance as usual I guess. That snarky attitude. Think I haven't heard it before? Talking is important, builds rapport with the customer. Plus talking makes the experience go by faster. And a fast transaction is a happy transaction! So, no, I will not stop talking. You want this procedure then you listen. I don't provide these discounted services because I can afford to. I do it because the only ones who can afford it are street-dumb kids who found themselves going the wrong direction. Ol' Proto here doing the good work."

"I'm not part of a gang."

"Kid. I know how it is. I can see you're not covered in the insignia and tatts, but you did cop a pulse blast. Like I said, I ask no questions, but I know shit. You think you're on the outside of it, but you're in deep. Just because the boys like having their fun with you at night doesn't mean you're protected. I'll say something and if I'm right you give me a little nod. You were with one of the members, maybe the leader, after enjoying some exercise if you know what I mean. Just chilling in their base, or lair, or whatever young idiots call them now when another gang hit. But this other gang is serious. This isn't a beatdown, this is a full-on statement of intent. Use of E.M.P. devices and everything. All the people you know are now ineffective and the full mechanicals are proper' fragged. Other gang then just strolls in, zeroing everyone. They see you, and you see them mulling it over in their heads, but whatever happens then you get let go. Cause' you're here now."

Sarah shook her head. "I'm not in a gang. I'm serious. I just need system reactivation."

Ol' Proto let out a mechanical sigh. "Suit yourself." He turned away from Sarah towards a small computer he had connected the other end of the input cables to. "I hope you're as tough as you try to appear. I'm sending a burst charge through you to reignite the biocells that power your gear. Think of it like a jump start. It's going to hurt, and you'll feel your heart beat out of sync. That's probably the worst part."

Before Sarah responded Ol' Proto flicked a switch and Sarah's body convulsed. Her heart felt like it burst inside her chest as every muscle in her body tensed and tightened. Her vision danced with holographic symbols, loading images of her systems starting their initialisations. The current continued through her body. "It's loading," she managed to get through her clenched teeth.

"Just a little bit longer. If we stop now they won't have the charge to stay on." Ol' Proto was focused on reading his terminal's display. "Seem's your persec is quite the hungry mod."

Sarah continued to endure the pain. She was trapped in her own skin as her body tightened and her muscles refused to relax. She would scream if her mouth could open any wider and her throat would soften. When her body did slump in the chair she didn't register it straight away.

"You're all set now. Make sure you perform some system checks before you try to stand up. If there's any issues tell me. I mean that. You don't tell me of any errors and you leave then trust me you'll regret it. Too many people think it's alright, it's a minor error and off they go. All spooked by the shock, not knowing that error is draining their charge again. Got to make sure the system can support itself again fully."

Sarah nodded while her vision danced. She closed her eyes, groaning as she readjusted herself in the seat. She began a system check on herself. Each modification and application returned green marks of success. She gave Ol' Proto a thumbs up.

"Next step is to connect to the Society and connect a media to me. Audio, visual, whatever, let's make sure your connection is working though."

"Ah, one second," Sarah hesitated. The outside of the building may have been designed to look like an office but this was clearly inside Ol' Proto's garage. She had seen his advertisement in the form of neon graffiti on the street walls, and Ol' Proto himself wasn't exactly clean looking. "Do you, or anyone you might know, have the ability to mask Society addresses?"

Ol' Proto chuckled happily. "Mask? Or do a full rewrite?"

"Full rewrite."

"Oh happy day!" Ol' Proto clasped his metal hands together. "I'm so glad you feel that way. Nothing better than a fresh start. This is your chance to walk away from that life and really make something of yourself now. There's more out there to life than just running in some gang.

You seem to be confident of yourself, something I see in a lot of gang side pieces. You could use that edge and make a lot of money being a skin cam model."

"No thanks," Sarah replied softly.

"That's alright. It's not for everyone. What other stuff might you like? Tell me, what did you want to be when you were little?"

"I didn't really think about it much. I liked pretending to sell stuff, or convincing people to buy stuff." She realised she was speaking in double. Her body was still calming after the shock.

"Advertisements. Respectable field. But awfully hard to get into. However I'm glad you're leaving crime behind you, so I will set you up. It's my way of giving back to the community. I like to try do a good deed every now and then. And before you ask, it's not about repenting or paying back for my previous life. I just like to help. It's my nature. Took me a while to figure it out, but I'm glad I did. So you see it's never too late to make a fresh start. Marketing, that's good. People got to know what to buy, and it's one of the easier inserts. Don't expect it to be just handed to you though, it's just a foot in the door. I'll rewrite some port access, give you a new Society address and identity, one with some *experience* in advertising. My one rule though, is you don't get to choose your new name. You don't get to choose your original name so why should this be any different? And don't worry, I'm not fond of those ugly names. But what I choose is final, a lot of it depends on the rewrite. Some names are easier to code than others."

"Didn't you choose Ol' Proto? I don't get any say at all?"

"That name was given to me by my customers. It suits, don't you think?"

"I guess."

"Some people say you grow into your name. As if it changes how you develop. I definitely grew old at least."

"You don't look too old. You dribble on like one though."

Ol' Proto chuckled again. "Watch out little one, you just may end up being called some fossil name yourself." He closed a window on his terminal. "We're almost done here. Just some more finishing touches and, ta-da. So, Mia, welcome to your new life."

"Mia? I hate it."

"Mia Rhodes. Be happy, I had an alternative for a Mai May. And I thought I wouldn't do any numbered names. You're going for a background with advertising now, better keep it somewhat classy. Mia it is."

"Mia Rhodes," Sarah, now Mia, repeated it aloud to herself.

"So, was there anything else today Mia?"

"Um, yeah. So I have a new Society access address?"

"Yep. Brand spanking new."

"What about my old contacts and settings?"

"Contacts I can move over. Any old accounts you held online though are closed off now."

"My b-card and fundbyte levels?"

"Still work, but if anyone checks now they'll register you as Mia Rhodes. That card belongs to whoever you were before. Might cause some legal issues for you if you take my meaning. My advice, leave it all behind. You got to break that habit of who you were. Only move forward, you know? And cut your connections to them other gang members, if any are still around. I only do these once for each customer, so I better not see you again claiming you fragged up and need another restart or format."

Sarah nodded. "Thank you, Proto."

Ol' Proto escorted Sarah off the chair and led her back out the front of the garage. "There's a cyberport cafe a few blocks down that way," he said pointing. "You should check for postings in the marketing sector. You won't have any problems applying, let them corporations fact check you, they are going to do it anyway. The history I've attached to you will make it smooth diving."

"Your *sign* said low cost. What do I owe?"

Ol' Proto smirked. "That was before the rewrite. Recharging purged systems is low cost, but the rewrite kind of messes with that. If people take me up on my second chance offer I tend to be a bit lenient. After all, you can't use your old b-card now can you? Tell you what, get your-self started and when you're a big marketing Executive, give Ol' Proto some free advertising."

"Deal." Sarah shook his metal hand and thanked him again. She walked in the direction of the cafe Ol' Proto had mentioned. She got two blocks before turning around and seeing if Ol' Proto had returned to the inside of his business. With no sign of him, she leant on the front wall of a building wall and cried.

She went through her contact list, all twelve of them. She had always believed it was a social sign of status not having too many contacts, just millions of followers. Yet now, brushed up against the wall of an organic pill dispensary she felt entirely alone. She looked over Cho's information, a whole friendship reduced down to a few lines of code and Society handshake keys. Most of their interactions had been Cho contacting her, rarely the other way around.

She scrolled to the brief data she had taken from Iskomo, nestled into her firmware by O.M.T. informant subscription settings. His panel just listed his Society address, the image remained blank. Sarah realised she almost wished he had at least taken the time to upload something, anything at least. Something to remember him by. Even if he had managed to send her something before the E.M.P. took out her systems, she was not Sarah Blackwell anymore.

Iskomo's data noted that he was online. Sarah remembered Iskomo constantly complaining about his faulty gear, the glitches and his fossil way of not knowing a damn thing about Society life. This was just another error of his. His society access key frozen and remained lagged in. She kept watching it, waiting for the online status to change to offline for the final time. She would witness it. She felt she owed him that much at least.

The wait continued. Sarah began to grow impatient, something she did feel guilty at recognising. "One last message at least." She whispered to herself. She chose text, as that seemed to be his preferred method.

I guess at least you tried. Thanks for that. I think I'm just going to go now. Bye Iskomo. And sorry I was a bitch.

She sent it off and closed her Society windows. She entered the pill dispensary and ordered a fruit salad protein. She had it charged to her Society account wirelessly, not risking using the physical b-card this early. The transaction processed, her new identity must have had some funds to begin with. Sarah wondered if she should have left her card with Ol' Proto. The wired techhead would flip if he had discovered the amount of fundbytes resting in that account. She took the pill from the wall slot when it flashed her number and threw it into the back of her mouth. Her Society link alerted her she had received a new message.

It would be just another notification of her purchase of the protein, she opened the notification without checking it's sender ready to delete it. She paused when she read the contents.

Who the frag is this? Iskomo had replied.

16

"I guess I don't quite understand what's happened, but I'm so fragging happy to see you," Sarah said. After the initial confusion and a
sceptical back and forth with Iskomo, he had agreed to meet her in one
of the billion Society chat forums. They had at least agreed on N0DE,
one of the less popular forums but with still enough traffic to not stand
out. The area was constructed as a large oval shaped dome where hundreds of people conversed or shared data. Along the walls were hundreds
of doors leading to subforums, special areas where users chatted about a
specific topic. A ring-like balcony circled above the main area, filled with
booth-like spaces where visitors could hold private chats.

Sarah had organised the use of one of the private chat spaces herself.
She set a password for entry, auto-generated by her systems that she
didn't bother noting down. Instead she sent Iskomo a direct invite to
the room. As she had correctly assumed, Iskomo had trouble relocating
himself to N0DE and had happily accepted the direct port. There, in
the safety of the private booth they had both exchanged tense questions
before settling on each other being the real deal.

"And you think I do?" Iskomo was still using the O.M.T. supplied
skin. He opened a vidfeed link using a floating window and showed
Sarah the footage he had found earlier.

"I know Iskomo," Sarah responded, closing it before the clip showed
the bullets delivered to Iskomo's body. "I was close by. I thought you
were dead."

"As far as I know, I should be. I know I'm new to all this deep dive
stuff, but I thought if your physical body died, you died."

"It does. Well at least I thought so," Sarah opened a search prompt
within the booth. "Maybe it's happened before. People die all the time
in dives, starving themselves by staying logged on for days at a time.

They all just seem to log out and never return. I've never heard of some-one continuing to live inside the Society." The search returned results of theories and new age websites, but no actual hits to explain what hap-pened. "There's nothing like this, anywhere. Do you realise the extent of what you've done? Somehow, you've like, downloaded your whole mind or something into the Society." She purposely gave her Society avatar a distrusting facial expression. "You're not really some android or something, are you?"

"Be serious," warned Iskomo. "You've seen me bleed. Frag, remem-ber the first time you met me? You mentioned the smell. Androids and that don't stink. One of the perks of being partial to real alcohol."

"Real? That stuff will fry your brain."

"That's what McCavern used to warn me. You think this has some-thing to do with that?"

"How the frag would I know? This is like a first. I don't even know what the repercussions of something like that would be. Just, I'm so fragging relieved you're still here."

"You said that already. Right now I'm more concerned with finding a way out of the Society." Iskomo said. He kept scanning Society links to anything that came close to independent conscious uploading. "If they did zero my body, and it sure looks that way, how am I ever to exit?"

"Does this mean you're some kind of virtual intelligence now? Or a virus?"

"Sarah, help me. I'm not either of those. I'm still me. Pretty sure I am at least. I'm definitely not a virus, O.M.T. security systems didn't even seem to register me."

Sarah checked the private chat panel. It listed the occupants of the booth as a single person. "Oh wow. Yeah I see. Even the chatroom pro-grams aren't counting you here. That's weird considering I could send you an invite through the system."

"I can still interact with prompts though," Iskomo said. For the first time, Sarah believed she heard a nervousness in his voice. "You know what, we should work this out later. Here." Iskomo presented the files of the Avery employees he'd found earlier. "These are no good to me stuck in here. Have a look at these."

"What am I looking for?" Sarah studied the data, lost.

"These three here all worked in upper management close to Alex Hughes. Two are dead and one might be missing. You had a link to someone with the same name, and at the same company, and you were targeted too. This Hughes is the centre of it."

"So we need to check their files."

"This is them. When O.M.T. takes over a new holding; they move everything to their own servers. We won't learn anything new. I need to talk to that Alex Hughes again." Iskomo slumped into the virtual seat of the booth. "My fragging body."

"Why is that? You just said the guy is zeroing people. What makes you think you could walk out of another meeting with him? They dropped a fragging bomb on us Iskomo!"

"I just need access to his personal terminal. Get something damning and puncture-proof. Then I could log it with the higher-ups at O.M.T. and clear all this shit up."

"You just said you were running under O.M.T.'s own security radars. And it's not registering you here, why not get into his personal terminal now? Online? While you're still, I don't know what to call you, a ghost? Spectre? You could port in, have a dig and leave without any access logs."

"How am I meant to find the location of that one terminal in all this?" Iskomo's arms waved around their surroundings. "There are too many sites and locations for me to even begin working out where to start."

"I see," Sarah nodded. "What you need is a way to ping the actual terminal so you can find it online."

"Whatever the frag that means. I need someone who can physically sit at it and pass the data to me."

"I can do it." Sarah volunteered.

"Don't be stupid kid. You wouldn't make it up the elevator."

"Look at me Iskomo." Sarah bit back. "I'm not Sarah anymore. This is Mia Rhodes. I got fragging scrubbed thinking I had to vanish. As far as their systems will know I'll be little unknown Mia."

"He'd recognise you. You haven't changed your physical appearance."

"Would he? I don't even know what this guy looks like!"

Iskomo felt drawn to Sarah's remark. "Wait," he said slowly, letting his thoughts form. He went through all his stored data on Sarah's case. It surprised him how much faster it was to take in the data online. "The courier who killed your roommate Cho. He at first thought it was you. He changed his story when I revealed he had killed her instead. The O.M.T. agent who started all this, what happened right before he attacked you?"

"Um. He asked me my name."

"Right," Iskomo was nodding. "No one actually could perfectly recognise you. They must have been only going on a name, maybe a location and some short notes about appearance." He stood up and began pacing in the booth. "No hits on your TG Boston account though. When did you start that?"

"About three years ago." Sarah watched him as he walked.

"I mean, did you start that after Alex, your ex, left?"

"I left her."

"Not important, just give me the timeline."

"Yeah, it was after we split. I needed the income."

"I think. I think this Alex has somehow slipped into your Alex's identity, and is now zeroing people who had ties to the original."

"That's fragged up, but it makes sense." Sarah said. "Holy shit it makes perfect sense! We need to get to that terminal!"

"You won't be able to just go in and get access or a meeting. I'm O.M.T. and they were reluctant. Need a plan."

"Mia is in advertising and marketing. Maybe I can go in and apply for a position."

"You'll still need an appointment." Iskomo stopped pacing, he noticed a complete lack of dizziness.

"I'll go in, when I get to the lobby terminal, I'll try to contact you. Maybe you can slip through a file or something saying I have a meeting. Don't worry about my credentials, Ol' Proto promised me they were solid."

"Who?"

"Just a guy. Did my scrub. Think you can manage that?"

"I can try to mock something up. Just be careful. Maybe just the lobby will be enough of a foot in the door."

"Alright. I'll head there now," Sarah vanished from Iskomo's view. Her voice continued to reach him, "Have that notice of meeting ready to send. I'll call you just before I ping the lobby."

"Be careful," Iskomo put it as a request.

"Iskomo."

"Yeah?"

"You lost your arm, and now your fragging whole body. For what it's worth. I'm sorry."

"Noted."

17

Sarah thought she'd be more nervous as she entered the Avery building. It had been a few hours since her online conversation with Iskomo and she wondered how he was keeping busy stuck in the Society. She had encouraged him to practice interacting with different prompts and systems, and much to his confusion he had mastered them with ease.

His first test at moving through security measures had occurred back at N0DE. He attempted to access a private V.I.P. lounge and change the display without being noticed. Without any need to interact or change any coding, he had simply walked through the security door and into the room. Iskomo then informed Sarah he had somehow already gained access to administrator controls and tried changing the wall design. Cyber security measures moved to intercept his location yet when they reached his position he reported they stood by idle. It wasn't until one of the users in the lounge saw the phenomenon that Iskomo left the space.

If he could handle that, he should be able to handle a copy paste of an appointment memo into the Avery employment server. Sarah had considered the option of trying to find some actual hardware to protect herself with in case things went sideways. In her mind though she heard Iskomo's grumbling about her elevated persec system and chose to rely on that. As she approached the lobby terminals she had to pass under weapon screening cameras, she took a deep breath at having made the smart choice.

"Mia Rhodes," she told the terminal as it logged her into the building's occupants. She didn't have any cards of identification to swipe so the machine prompted her for Society credentials. She acknowledged the privacy agreements and refused the mailing list sign up. The terminal then requested access to her Society which she accepted. As her system handshaked with the terminals, she sent Iskomo a short written message. If he could trace the source quickly, he may be able to get the rough location of Avery's server in time. She just hoped he was ready and didn't miss it.

The terminal welcomed her as Mia Rhodes and asked her purpose for the visit. She quickly made an online call to Iskomo. "Are you close?"

"I think. This is disorientating as shit." His gruff voice came back. "I think, here. Do I just drop this?"

"Iskomo?"

"Give it a go."

Sarah turned her attention back to the terminal. "Interview. Marketing?" She cursed herself for making it sound like a question.

The lobby terminal prompted a please wait notification and searched it's own database. As it passed one second of searching Sarah started to feel uneasy at the time it was taking. She heard Iskomo swear about something and realised he was still connected. "What's going on?"

"There's way too much stuff going on in here. I'm being hit with control windows everywhere."

The terminal screen changed to an error. Appointment found but a Human Resources officer is not present currently. The terminal continued to direct her to reschedule.

"Check again," Sarah asked. "I can wait in the lobby." She walked away from the terminal, hoping to force its acceptance.

"Get to the elevator," Iskomo's voice came through.

"Now?"

"Yes, now."

Sarah walked to the elevators, the one closest to her opening its doors as she approached. "Iskomo? This you?"

"The terminal system seems to be looping. I think I can send you up to Alex's floor using this elevator."

"Are we actually doing this? Still haven't been able to pinpoint the correct one?" Sarah stood inside the elevator as it began rising. She couldn't help but notice the disrepair of the small area she was in. It was the first elevator she'd experienced that groaned as it moved, the holographic display on the interior doors had been smashed and were inoperable.

"There's so many sub sections here. It's like a maze. Listen, the floor I'm sending you to had rows and rows of computers. One belonged to Jody Banks, it'll still be empty. Find it and send me something from it. Might make my search a bit quicker if I know which section those servers are."

The elevator doors opened and Sarah stepped into the large room Iskomo described. Rows of terminals stretched to the opposite wall, each joined by a heavily padded cushion chair where they could sit plugged in. "Shit."

"What? What?"

"Iskomo, this whole place is empty." Sarah stood in the quiet room. "How am I to know which one was Jodie's?"

"Just pick any one then," Iskomo urged her.

Sarah ran to the first terminal she saw and got into the chair. She took the cable and plugged it into the back of her neck where her Society port was. "What if it needs a log in?"

"Then you don't know the corporate world very well." Iskomo responded.

Sarah activated the port and dived into the terminals Society hub. A floating message was waiting for her as she found herself standing before the Avery logo.

New user. Log in created. Welcome to your new life at Avery Mia Rhodes!

"That simple?" Sarah didn't believe what had just processed.

"You think people want to bother themselves putting in paperwork and stuff? All these places are streamlined now. Plus when O.M.T. took over they would have installed the instant logins just to speed up the transition. The merger happened two days ago, maybe three. I can't tell the time anymore. They keep these programs equipped for a week at least."

"So can you trace me here?"

"Send an actual file, I'll try do what I did last time."

"How did you work it out? You managed to source Avery pretty fast."

"Honestly? I really don't know, but it seems to be working whatever I'm doing."

Sarah sent Iskomo another written message, she filled it with nonsense and hit the send prompt. "Get it?"

"Frag me, over there?" Iskomo sounded disappointed. "I wasn't even close."

"Should I look for anything?" Sarah asked.

"Check for any posts from people in a supervisor posi-" Iskomo's voice was cut short. Sarah's vision went white and her head felt like it was spinning. She reached out a hand to steady herself and felt the cushion chair she sat upon.

She blinked her eyes repeatedly trying to bring her senses back. She had been booted from the Society again, the abruptness of it made her dizzy. Slowly her focus came back and she saw a man in a grey business suit standing over her, the Society jack hanging from his hand.

"Who are you?" he asked while staring at her.

"Mia Rhodes," Sarah responded, rubbing the back of her neck. Her sense of taste was coming back as she tried to speak. "I started today."

"You are incredibly early," the man stated back at her. He dropped the cable in his hand and crossed his arms. "I hadn't received any notice of new staff joining us this week. What are you up to?"

"I'm sorry sir," Sarah rubbed her eyes. "I just wanted to make a good impression. Carol got me this job and I didn't want to make her look bad. I thought if I got here early and set up my account it would save time."

The man nodded as he listened. He said something to Sarah she couldn't understand with Iskomo demanding his own answers to her sudden absence again. She politely nodded herself, smiling weakly.

"I said come with me," the man ordered. "Not a very good first impression now is it if you don't listen."

Sarah jumped out of her seat, apologising. The man led her further past the rows of terminals to an office at the back. Inside he motioned for her to have a seat. Her eyes were still fuzzy and strained with the many lights glittering from the wall of servers behind the man as he sat down.

"Do you always pull out your employee's jacks like that?"

"What are you doing here?" the man asked her again. "I don't buy your story for an instant. Using some dodgy program to try slip an appointment into my servers. You a spy sent by a rival competition? Whose your real employer?"

"What?"

"I'm Alex Hughes, and I run all the tech here at Avery. Nothing gets past me. Is it Technix? It is, isn't it? Wondering why O.M.T. just signed this place. Well you can wonder all you want in lockdown. Confess and I may just put in a good word with metro. Don't, and well, I know people at O.M.T. who like to get information their own way."

"I told you my name is Mia Rhodes." Sarah insisted. Sarah ignored Iskomo's voice jabbering in her mind and internally began to overcharge her persec system. Warning messages flashed in her vision as she felt her hairs begin to stand on end.

"I can say whatever Technix promised to pay you is not worth it." Alex Hughes flashed her a wicked grin.

Sarah had enough, her body felt electrified. She pounced off her chair and reached for Alex across the desk. She grabbed him by the hand as he tried to pull away. He freed himself and looked at her surprised. "My persec?" Sarah was just as confused.

"Your persec? Why you, wait," Alex's eyes widened as he stared at her. "You're Blackwell!"

"Iskomo!" Sarah screamed vocally and internally, sending the audio in all directions she could on the Society.

Alex dived for his desk and hit something on his terminal. Panels on the office ceiling opened and security hardware dropped from them. Two black plated weapons with barrels the size of Sarah's arms spun as their lasers swept the area for a target. Sarah dived for the ground covering her head as she heard the machines begin to activate and target her. Gunfire echoed in her ears briefly, the noise so loud it was impossible to hear anything else. Sarah was sure she was still screaming as the rattle died off.

She lay on the floor, waiting for the pain to kick in. She had heard rumours that it hurts less if you don't look at your wounds. She waited, feeling numb but nothing else. In her head she heard Iskomo telling her to get up.

"My persec didn't work on him," she told Iskomo who wouldn't shut up. "I thought I could, it doesn't matter. My original account had a lot of fundbytes saved. You should take it. The secondary access password is TGBoston1. I know, but the simplest passwords are the least suspected."

"Frag sake kid you're not hit. Get the frag up!" Iskomo's voice was furious.

Sarah pushed herself off the floor. The turrets hanging on the ceiling followed her movement as she stood up. She stared into their sensors, "Iskomo?"

"What the frag were you thinking?"

"I said it! My persec! A quick shock then an even quicker getaway. It didn't work on him either." She looked over to where Alex had been standing. The desk had been chipped and damaged by the turrets. From her angle she could see Alex's shoes coming from behind the desk with a growing pool of red. "Did you?"

"Yes. You are fragging lucky. I saw the security program activate and managed to get control of it just as it was lining you up. I feel physically sick."

"No one feels anything online. But, thank you Iskomo." Sarah sat back down in the chair. She held her arms together trying to settle the shaking.

"You need to get out of there before the office fills up. I'm deleting the visitor logs and security vidfeeds. Pick yourself up kid."

"Did you find anything?"

"Yes," Iskomo replied, "and then some."

18

"This was on Alex's personal terminal. It's a file detailing something they refer to as standard insertion procedure." Iskomo copied the file over to Sarah. They had reloaded into Iskomo's personal Society hub again.

Sarah noticed he still hadn't changed any of the default settings. Yet the file he sent transferred to her immediately. "Looks like you're sort of getting the hang of this. So what's in this?" She activated the file and loaded it's contents into a floating window between them.

"It seems to detail some key interactions in Alex's life. Your Alex's. As far as I can tell it's been limited to just this city though. Look, there, your name as a previous associate. Then there's these three; Jason Breckinridge, Ciaran Amos and Eleri Cressmont. I found their names also on the O.M.T. server with a hidden hyperlink I couldn't follow. However those files came from Avery too."

"Is this enough?" Sarah clicked on her name in the window. "It's barebones. It just lists me as a potential identifier. It doesn't even say we were together. What the frag is this too? Minimal threat?"

"It's enough," Iskomo closed the window on Sarah. "If there is one thing O.M.T. hates, it's bad press. And especially during the quarterly coming up. If I can get this to the Heads they'll deal with it quickly."

Sarah stood silently, watching Iskomo as he talked. He noticed her apprehension.

"They love good press even more. They also care about statistics. Numbers and figures they can show strength with. Which is what they'll do. They can mark this case closed, add it to the success pile and bump those numbers up. They'll have some sort of project deep in research and development, cloning or something. This could be cloning. They could give me my body back, my full body."

"Iskomo," Sarah cut him off. "I think you're spiralling or some-thing."

"Why? Because I want my fragging body back? Because I'm so close to getting offline again? This is it, right here," he pointed at the data he held. "This makes it over."

"What about me?" Sarah raised her voice. "I gave up my identity! I had fans, I had success! The only thing I've gotten from all this is a seri-ous distrust of anyone from a corporation. The news lady, the one who just stood by while some others zeroed your ass. Her, yeah the stuff she was saying seemed to be coming straight from your buddies at O.M.T! Don't go there Iskomo. Take it somewhere else, take it to that Dagesh guy you made me see."

"He has no authority over O.M.T. He's just part of some suburban private security force. The only way I can end this is to take it to man-agement."

"It can be ended though. Right now. You say that file links Alex to the attempt on me? Well we got him. You got him. Filled him right up with the justice he deserved in his office. That's good enough for me."

"Are you listening? I'm fragging trapped here, I got no fragging body!"

"I'll try to reach out to some of my fans, I'm sure there are some se-rious kitters in there. Maybe someone will know more about your situ-ation. Just don't go."

"I'm going." Iskomo began to leave the small hub.

"What if it's easier to just delete you?" Sarah called after him. "If I was some prick obsessed with company image that's what I'd do."

Iskomo paused and looked over his shoulder at her. His avatar's ex-pression still a blank image with O.M.T. coding over it. He let out a deep sigh and raised his palms to his face. "I'm so tired. Like I've been think-ing too long. I don't know if sleeping is even possible in here, I can't seem to cover my eyes for a moment's darkness. Deletion wouldn't be so bad."

"What? Not everything on the Society is so illuminated! There's plenty of sites with dark aesthetics. There's virtual nightclubs."

"And be forced to listen to shitty rave music being blasted? My mind's made up."

"You're an idiot!"

"No!" Iskomo shouted back at her. "I'm experienced. And I'm fragging lucky. Everything I do reeks of it. I couldn't even die right. Just my luck, popping up again and trapping me here. You know when I was wandering the Society, unable to contact you that I thought I was dead? That this was my punishment, stuck in the one place I could never stand? I couldn't have imagined a more fitting punishment."

"If they don't delete you they'll stick you in some contained server. Kept offline. Study you and find out how you managed this separation. Trust me, I wanted nothing but revenge earlier but maybe this is it. Maybe we should just take it and go."

"Goodbye," Iskomo cut her off and with a wave of his hand, emitting a large pulse. Sarah found herself disconnected from the Society.

"Motherfragger!" She cursed aloud removing the cable from her neck. The other patrons in the cybersuites not connected took a moment to look at her, then looked away again. Sarah rubbed her eyes and let the disorientation fade.

A female attendant approached her. She wore a black skull t-shirt and her movement was smooth due to the wheels at the base of her mechanical legs. "I get it, but please don't disturb the other users."

Sarah scoffed at the woman, raising to her feet. "Get what? You don't get shit. Some people have actual problems."

The woman scowled. "You need to vacate the premises. A rideshare has already been called."

Sarah flipped her off and left the business. Outside she spotted a street peddler sitting on the curb, his wares assorted onto a blanket on the pavement. He looked up at her blankly, a cigarette hanging from his mouth.

"Got another one of those?" She asked him.

The street peddler nodded. "Yeah. But uh, twenty fundbytes for the igniter, yeah?"

"Just give it to me," Sarah ordered. Why was everyone in this city such a fraghead. She took the cigarette from the peddler's thin, outstretched hand. "Thanks." She took out her original b-card and waved it over the peddler's ancient device.

"Thanks!" The peddler gave her a toothy grin.

Sarah ignited the tip of the cigarette and drew the smoke into her lungs. It was harsh but she suppressed the cough.

"Bad day?" the peddler asked.

"Looks to be a bad week. Last three days have been absolutely fragged."

"You look to be well off enough. Could always be worse."

"Listen pal, you don't have the slightest idea what I'm going through. Do the decent thing like everyone else and mind your own business." Sarah took another drag.

The peddler chuckled to himself, still sitting cross legged behind his display.

"Something amusing?" Sarah began to doubt the chemical composition of the cigarette.

"It's just an odd thing to say."

Sarah watched the peddler closely. The man had a beard that hadn't yet fully grown in, revealing the fact his face once sported a goatee appearance. While he looked fallen on hard times, his clothing was in better condition than other street peddlers she'd seen before. "How so?"

"People don't want other people to mind their business," the peddler leant back against the front wall of the cybersuites.

"Yes they do," Sarah argued. "Just look around here, no one pays any attention to anyone else. You're full of shit."

"Out here maybe, but that's only because the culture has shifted online now. It's obvious on the Society."

Sarah shrugged and risked another drag on the cigarette. "What? Explain it to me then."

The peddler flashed a grin, "Even my wisdom isn't free." He nodded at her b-card again. "Ten more fundbytes I'll let you in on the secret of human nature."

"Just another scam artist then is it?" Sarah checked the sky above the street, still no sign of the rideshare that had been supposedly called. "Frag it. Let's see what you got." She swiped her b-card again, allowing the fundbyte exchange. "Out with it."

"Well, people don't really want people to mind their own business. My theory is that humans have this *need* to be watched. They want to be popular, or famous, they want the fans."

Sarah grew uncomfortable. She checked the street for any signs of danger.

"Think of it this way. Early days of mankind, same strange need to be witnessed. What do they come up with? Gods. Up there somewhere, something is watching you. That's how they got the connection they needed so bad. And that works well enough for the first few centuries, but soon even that is not enough. People need actual realisation of attention. So it shifts. Now it's about being famous, a rock star of the old days or the old vidfeed features. The Great Dream they called it. Be a celebrity and everyone will watch and want to know you. Then we get even smarter. We make those early networks and now everyone has a voice. Those early social media platforms, blogs and websites all hosting thousands and thousands of people's musings. Every day taking to it to update their content, stay relevant, stay watched. They could count their views and that's what drove it all, it's still the same today. It's just more immersed within the Society now. These people don't need to be noticed out here, as long as they're noticed in there. As long as there is at least one subscriber it fills that primal need of theirs. Who knows where it'll go next."

"Holy shit," Sarah stared at the man.

"I'm right, aren't I? Blew your mind yes?"

"Who the frag are you?"

The man motioned at the hardware set out in front of him. "Just a man trying to make a living selling junk."

"Bullshit. Tell me." Sarah dropped the cigarette and stubbed it out with her shoes. A rideshare vehicle set down beside her on the street, the doors opening for her.

"I was involved in theory and culture studies with Sandgate University. You know it? It was just another corp posing as education." The peddler protected his blanket of wares from being blown away by the descending rideshare's thrusters. "I developed class unit programs there. Well, not anymore. But hey, that's big business for you, always quick to replace you."

"Frag," Sarah uttered, "I just worked it out." She thanked the peddler for the smoke and quickly got into the rideshare.

"Where to? You haven't uploaded any directions," the driver muttered from the front seat.

"O.M.T. offices," Sarah said, "And quickly."

19

Iskomo found himself back in the O.M.T. databank server easily enough. There was no more lag but his mind still felt slow. He hadn't paused by the log-in terminal, passing it instead to enter the sealed virtual space without issue. He drifted towards the financial records and pulled out the first file he found.

With it in hand, he could see the various links into the darkness of cyberspace. They appeared to him like neon ribbons stretching to another room at a vast distance. He could identify clearly past the darkened space between, barriers created by the Society to separate different areas for its users and programmers. He tugged on a red neon one linking to a manager's cache. The sensation of being pushed and pulled filled his senses as the new location built itself around him.

The small space of data belonged to a name Iskomo didn't recognise. He flipped through the different postings and information littered about the cache. Iskomo worked his way to find an in-house O.M.T. messenger service. The room pulsed, which he ignored. A room-wide laser scanned the entire area, once again passing through Iskomo as if he wasn't there. Before it had finished it's cycle, Iskomo had found an outgoing message to a chat group consisting of heads of departments. He activated the source of that link and flowed towards the next area.

The small forum featured a circular table with seats situated around it. Iskomo groaned at the sight of it. Typical of suits to think themselves higher than their stations. The centre of the table held a prompt that would alert the members of the group to any called meetings. Iskomo compiled his collected data on Alex Hughes and the rest of Avery and slotted it into the table's coding. Another laser beam swept the room, with another failure to register his presence. Dulled, but feeling ready regardless, he pinged the centre prompt of the table calling the meeting.

The first two arrived at the same time, both whom Iskomo didn't recognise. Both were clean shaven, with carefully designed digital hair. Their online avatars appeared almost human. Iskomo wondered how much skins like that cost. They saw him standing there in the room with them yet ignored him, taking seats at the table. Another perfectly designed avatar came in, who Iskomo recognized as one of the females who handled the outgoing accounts. She sat turn and leant over to one of the first two. "Clemens, Simmons, why is there a base level investigator in our chat?" she asked them quite loudly, her eyes not leaving Iskomo.

The fourth was Lad Winters. The face of O.M.T. press releases. He took his seat without acknowledging anyone in the room. "There was no session scheduled for now. There better be a damn good reason for this. I'm in the middle of a meeting with representatives for the quarterlies results." He finally noticed Iskomo. "What's he doing here?"

Iskomo didn't wait for anymore to log in. "Mr Winters. I have data here-."

"Stop," Winters interrupted him. "Where is your department head? Someone get, what's his name, McCreedy in here."

"I think you should see this," Iskomo carried on regardless. He activated the table, the data opening in a large floating screen above it. "During a case I was tasked with I uncovered sensitive information regarding Avery. A company recently acquired by O.M.T. There is evidence here of conspiracy and fraud."

"Explain," Winters coldly snapped. Iskomo noticed the arrival of a fifth person. The avatar was nowhere near as polished as the others but still resembled McCavern.

"This file on one Alex Hughes-" Iskomo was interrupted again.

"Not you," Winters dismissed Iskomo with a wave of his hand before pointing it at the woman. "You. You said he could handle the details. Get him synced in here to explain this fragging shit-show."

"Iskomo?" McCavern had read the identification codes on Iskomo's avatar and was manually inputting them somewhere. "How?"

"Can't connect," the woman Winters had berated announced.

Clemens spoke up next. "Avery has just filed a report," his eyes turned from Iskomo to the woman. "Robin, your son was just found dead in his office. Security system breach."

Robin's face drained of its colour. "What!" She screamed and brought her fists down on the table, the thud silent in the online chat. Her grief turned to fury and she turned on McCavern. "I ordered you to help him!"

McCavern took a step back, shocked. "Don't blame this on me! I had it under control! You're the one who took over my job and ruined it all!" McCavern approached Winters. "She uses her position, breaks into my office, and undoes everything with some fragshit about pesticides. Kills Brass in broad daylight at the same fragging time," He turned back to the woman, whose face seemed unnaturally tight. "Pro-tip for you, if you want to silence a media icon, don't do it with a fragging O.M.T. agent in direct contact with them! That shit still links us to it!"

The woman rose from her chair, marching towards McCavern, "You were supposed to train my son how to use it properly! This is all on you! I don't even know why you're part of these meetings!" Her voice was shrill, bordering on hysterical.

"Your son tried to hack one of my agents! Neals is still debugging from the mess he made!"

Winters shouted in frustration, silencing them both. "Fix this, and that," He motioned at Iskomo. "Close the whole thing. Anymore leaks and I'll auction your spots."

"Wait!" Iskomo called out but Winter's avatar vanished from the room. A pulse bounced through the room from the table, passing through each avatar present. Iskomo looked at McCavern, whose expression betrayed confusion. "Trying to purge me from the server?"

Another pulse emitted from the table. "Some kind of A.I?" McCavern muttered.

"Is this the agent?" Simmons spoke, rising from his own seat. "I thought he was retired."

Without missing a beat McCavern answered. "He was. That is his company supplied avatar though."

"You heard Mr Winters, sort it out. Robin, sorry for your boy," He then vanished along with Clemens.

"Delete him!" Robin ordered. Iskomo thought he saw actual rendered spit leave her lips.

"McCavern," Iskomo pulled his files back from the table's input. "It's really me. How are you part of this?"

"If it is really you," McCavern seemed focused on other tasks, "then you know you really fragged up this time." His hands seemed to move, shuffling code about too fast for Iskomo to see. "All you had to do was get the brat to give a public recant. I had it sorted."

"So you're going to delete me?" Iskomo held the data folder in his hand. "I know your family!"

"You're a tool. You were being let go anyway. Let's be honest, O.M.T. doesn't have retirement packages for investigators. More importantly, *how* are you here?" McCavern circled Iskomo like a shark. From the walls of the room four large glowing red translucent panels floated towards Iskomo.

"You can't trap me. No security systems work on me," Iskomo warned as the walls closed in on him. He went to move for the door, an exit link waiting to take him back to a previous server when the red panel shoved him backwards. Iskomo tried to pass through the panel and felt it resist his path. The four panels came together, sealing Iskomo in a small square space. Iskomo banged the walls with his fists, but his strikes produced not even sound.

McCavern gave a triumphant grin and approached the trapped Iskomo. "Clever. Didn't think you had the know-how. You're running your avatar on a lower rendering frequency than the rest of the Society."

Iskomo could hear Sarah's mocking voice in his head, *I told you so, I told you so.* He searched for any openings. Without a destination in mind he couldn't will himself through the floor or roof. He tried to buy himself more time. "I've sent this to Technix!"

McCavern shrugged from the other side of the panels. "I'm sure they do the same thing. I'm far more interested in how a dead man is still on-line." His right hand made a quick sweeping motion and Iskomo was flung into darkness.

20

"Hello.

And welcome to the Oil, Medical and Technology Informant Hotline Channel.

Please wait as we verify your connection mode.

Thank you. You are connected virtually. Please wait as we check your informant credentials.

It appears you are not a member of the O.M.T. informant members club. If you would like to create an account now, please say so.

All information is treated with dignity and respect. We respect your choice, but for safety concerns, our servers have logged and time-stamped your Society access address.

Did you know as a member of the O.M.T. informant members club you can track your submission in real-time? Members can also set up personal alerts to your case to see hourly updates. You also will be eligible to receive the benefits of our rewards program, where every fifth successful submission case closure pays double the reward value. You can apply for this service at any time.

Please state the reason for your visit today."

"I want to apply as an investigator." Sarah told the program.

"There are currently, sixteen, available positions for Informant Agents available. Transferring you to recruitment."

The small white room of the informant channel morphed as Sarah sat in the chair again. Three windows opened in front of her awaiting her selections. She interacted with each prompt, checking off boxes and scanning her identification into each. She electronically signed a non-disclosure agreement and chose the option for a face to face interview.

She took the available slot closest, set for half an hour's time with the head of the department, McCavern.

Confirmed, she disconnected from the Society from the public access terminal provided in the O.M.T. building lobby. She reached into her jacket pocket, checking her gear was still there. Her rideshare driver on the way over had stared at her too long from his cockpit. When he had asked if she was the TG Boston, her reaction had given it away. Luckily for her, he was a self-proclaimed true fan and had a million questions for her regarding her last update days ago. With some excuses, and a lot of flirting, Sarah had managed to get the driver to take her to his shady friends. There she had briefly posed for a picture with the driver and friend in exchange for an electromagnetic pulse grenade. It felt fitting to her as her form of revenge.

She steeled herself the following minutes as they passed. She had scored a large, puffy jacket from her rideshare's friend. Dark purple with the bright red graffiti *Get Sum* adorning its back. She kept her jacket collar up around her face, concealing it enough not to be suspicious. She avoided looking around, leaving the port cable resting on the back of her neck giving the appearance she was still plugged in. Soon her automated system messages alerted her to the scheduled meeting and she rose. She followed her navigation applications directions and was directed down a hallway. She followed it for some hundred metres, passing a team of janitors working on cleaning a dirtied wall. She caught a faint scent from the scene and was reminded of how Iskomo reeked when she first met him. Eventually she arrived outside a closed door, the name McCavern printed on it.

The door opened as she got closer and she heard a familiar voice telling her to enter and take a seat. She entered and recognised him instantly with his multiple ports hanging from the side of his head. His eyes remained focused on his terminal, his fingers tapping away at his table's inbuilt lightboard. She made no mistake, this was the same man who she had shocked in the incentive rooms. He barely registered her, not taking his eyes off his work.

"Is that how you dress for a position interview?" McCavern sneered out of the side of his mouth. "You don't look like much of a marketing manager. Tell me why you want to be an agent." His one human eye glanced over at her, briefly.

"And do you always show so much interest in your candidates?" Sarah quipped back. She mentally planned how to best produce the grenade.

"You can show yourself the door with that snark," McCavern continued typing. "What I'm doing right now is far more important than anything you'll ever amount to." He turned to give her a condescending stare, but his face became puzzled with recognition.

"Yeah, it's me motherfragger!" Sarah lunged forward and grasped at McCavern. Her movements were more carefully considered, so much so a brief thought entered her head; *I'm getting good at this.*

McCavern convulsed with the pain of the persec shock, falling to the floor free of Sarah's grasp. She exhaled, her heart pounding with the worry it would have had no effect. She swung her legs over the table and followed him down. She pressed her knee into his chest and ripped out the cords plugged into the side of his head with one firm tug. He groaned and his human eye rolled back into the skull. "Four disconnects at the same time? Must be a bitch," Sarah snarled. McCavern's head rocked side to side as he came out of the disorientation.

Sarah touched his forehead with her palm, sending another wave of electrical shock into him. If she could time it right, the techhead wouldn't have a time between charges to send an alert out. "Where's Iskomo? Has he been here?" Sarah sent another jolt into McCavern's body.

McCavern let out a throaty laugh through his clenched teeth. Sarah shocked him again and pulled out the E.M.P. grenade, holding it in front of McCavern's eye.

"Know what this is? Yeah you do. I bet you have so much hardware this would probably kill you. Not me though, my vitals aren't all interlinked with systems like you. Where is Iskomo?"

"You detonate that and you'll kill him too," McCavern groaned.

"So, he's here?" Sarah pressed her hand down hard on McCavern's head. She let the electricity shock continue to coarse through him until white foam came from his mouth. When she removed it, she also took her knee off from his chest. McCavern remained still but breathing.

She stood up to the terminal and checked the open programs. Most were reports and incoming data from agents on jobs, one appeared severed from any network and was compiling analysis data. Sarah couldn't make sense of it from the desktop display. She checked back to McCavern, still unmoving and saw the plugs sitting beside him on the floor. Without pausing, she clutched at one connected to McCavern's terminal and plugged it into the back of her neck.

She became surrounded with a three-dimensional world of McCavern's personal terminal. She found the analysis program and inspected it in the dived format. More options were available, including allowing it network access. She clicked yes and the program shattered before her eyes.

"Iskomo!" Sarah called as the avatar of Iskomo charged at her through the splintering prompt, yelling wildly. He saw Sarah and stopped.

"Kid?" He moved towards her quickly. "Wait how?"

"No time," Sarah said. "Get to another server somewhere on the Society. Anywhere. We need to get out of here!"

Iskomo stopped, turning his head towards another file. "Holy frag, that's it, all of it." He rushed to it and scanned it. "You need to take this with you!" He tried handing it to Sarah.

"Later!" Sarah pleaded.

"Wait, are you in O.M.T. right now?" Iskomo's eyes widened.

"Get out of here Iskomo! Go, give it to me later! I'll find you!" Sarah moved her hand to the back of her neck, ready to instant unplug.

"Wait!" Iskomo stopped her. "McCavern found out I was on some sub-channel or whatever he called it. He updated his programs so I can't leave this area." Iskomo tried prompting any of his previous links from his history. "See, I'm stuck here." His head turned as if listening to some far away conversation. "Run Sarah, alerts have just been issued throughout the O.M.T."

"Not without you!" Sarah yelled back and ran towards his avatar. "I'm so sick of your shit!"

"Not this again!" He waved his arms the same way he disconnected her earlier.

"No! You will not purge me away again!" Sarah screamed it in Iskomo's avatar's blank face and grabbed him by the hand as hard as she could. When the pulse hit her, forcing her back offline she continued to grip his hand.

She came back to reality still inside McCavern's office. She expected guards around her but from her view couldn't see any. She tried turning her head and found she was unable to move her neck. Even reaching her arm to pull out the port accomplished nothing, her arm remaining immobile.

Without her control, she watched helplessly from inside her mind as her body rose from the floor, looking around in a panic at the scene. *What the frag!* She screamed in her own mind.

Her body shuddered and her arms had moved to cup her ears. "Ow!" Her physical voice responded to the quiet room. She watched as her focus checked her hands and arms, then chest. Her hands moved down her body, padding her sides, legs and knees.

Her physical voice spoke again. "What the frag indeed."

Sarah, still helpless in her own skin, raised the question to herself. *Iskomo?*

"Yeah," her voice said, shaking.

I think I got you off the Society.

"I see that, but, but."

Looks like we're two minds sharing the one body. My fragging body. And you have total control.

21

There had been many nights in Iskomo's youth where he found himself staying awake well past the midnight hours drinking. Faces with names he couldn't recall but their conversations echoed faintly. Speculation of when, or even if technology could ever perfect transporting someone's mind into another body. They imagined themselves as drunk scholars, discussing the points and how it possibly could be achieved. These discussions always ended the same way, talking about the first thing they'd do if they found themselves in the body of the opposite gender.

The only thing Iskomo found himself enthralled with was the fitness of Sarah. She had no aching bones, no back pains, the energy of the youthful. He had forgotten the feel of a body that wasn't decaying from years of alcohol abuse. Even the air filling her lungs as he ran tasted different.

Where are you going?" Sarah's voice filled his mind. She had been forced to accept the situation but still reminded Iskomo of a backseat pilot.

"Out of here! I need to get this information to someone!" The sound of Sarah's voice projecting Iskomo's words still felt odd to him.

Iskomo ignored the alarms sounding throughout the building. He turned from the hallway into the lobby, ready to break for freedom. When he saw the security drone waiting in front of the doors with Neals directing visitors out of the building, he dived for cover behind a lobby terminal.

Shit! Did they see us?

Iskomo tilted Sarah's head and peeked around the edge of the terminal. Neals had been focused on the other hallway and had missed their entrance. The black armoured drone hovered idly mid-air on its twin mini-engines. Its long, elongated head was designed to always appear looking down at it's targets. Two arms stretched out from its headframe ending with small turrets and scanning arrays. It spun on its axis to face Iskomo and Sarah.

"Frag," Iskomo swore in unison with Sarah.

The drone fired a burst of non-lethal plascrete pellets at the terminal. The terminal sparked as the pellets ripped through the framework, riddling it with holes. Iskomo dived for more cover behind the wall of one of the public Society ports. He heard Neals yelling and the loud clanks of heavy security barriers falling to the ground, sealing the exit.

The drone flew forward to flank them, the short bursts from its engines calculated and precise. Iskomo kept Sarah's body moving, going around corners and any cover he could find as the drone tracked them. He risked popping her head up to see where Neals was. Iskomo saw him pushing to the right of the door, planning to catch them on his other flank.

"That drone will make scrap meat of us," Iskomo warned. He burst from his cover to the other side of the lobby, the drone firing at their heels.

I have a grenade! Sarah's voice came through clearly despite the gunfire and engine bursts. *Inside jacket pocket!*

Iskomo reached in and found it. "I can't use this, the drone is too close!" He rolled away from more cover to get behind a pillar, hoping the drone hadn't seen.

"Miss Blackwell! Give it up! Let's talk about this!" Neals yelled. He had shifted again, gun drawn. He was getting dangerously close again with the drone.

Iskomo ran again as the drone rounded the pillar, another salvo of pellets being fired. He ran for Neals, knowing the drone was programmed not to risk harming O.M.T. agents. Neals raised his gun. Iskomo ducked into a slide before he took his shot, Sarah's legs connecting with Neals' ankle. He tripped forward beside Sarah and Iskomo slid off her jacket, wrapping it around Neals' head. He felt the grenade in the jacket and tightened a fist around it from the outside material, feeling the click of activation.

Neals swore and fired his gun blindly. The drone came around from the pillar and approached the two. Iskomo knocked the gun from Neals, picking him up by the jacket wrap and shoved him towards the drone. Iskomo then ran further away from the two. The drone swerved right of Neals and fired another burst of pellets at Sarah, several which hit their target.

Each one felt like being hit by a rod. Sarah's voice cried out in pain at the same time. The small plascrete bullets had embedded themselves in Sarah's back, skin deep, knocking the air out of from them. Iskomo fell behind another set of walled seats.

Are we far enough?

A magnetic blast erupted from the jacket on Neals before Iskomo could answer. Neals yelled in muffled agony. The drone fell silent and hit the ground with a heavy crash. It skidded along the lobby floor connecting with Neals close to it. Its momentum sweeping his legs from under and his head hit the ground with a hard thud.

Get up, zero him!

"He wasn't aware, he was hacked previously." Iskomo argued.

He isn't now!

"No!" Iskomo checked himself over, he was still present in Sarah's body. He pushed himself to their feet, their back feeling damp with blood. Iskomo looked at the exit, still sealed behind the thick metal barriers. "Frag it," he muttered in her voice, "Plan B."

He hobbled to a door marked for employee's only, shoving it open to reveal a staircase. He descended, gripping the railing as Sarah's back burned.

Where does this go?

"Just let me get there first," Iskomo winced. He kicked open another door to enter a room of lockers. He approached one and entered a six-digit code into the panel, unlocking it.

Is this your locker?

"Pretty obvious isn't it?" Iskomo reached in and grabbed an O.M.T. branded jacket and hat. He covered Sarah's body with the new clothing and went back to the stairwell. "There's people all over this building. If we can't get out we may as well try to blend in. Might buy us some time." He continued deeper.

What happened Iskomo? Where did you go? How did they lock you in that program?

Iskomo groaned again. "It's in that file I grabbed. Plus McCavern thought explaining it would convince me to cooperate with him."

It's some kind of replacement system, isn't it?

"Yes, how did you...? Doesn't matter, we have evenmore evidence now. Because of over-population high end positions are rare. So when some kid of one of these wealthy suits comes along and wants a job, they make room."

Say it, Iskomo.

"That's what happened to your Alex. Apparently it's easier, and cheaper on the datawork to just send in the brat to pose as the previous. Zero the original, slot in the new and act as if it were them all along."

And I was a loose end.

"Yes. Because you could recognise your Alex. So could three of the supervisors who reported to Alex."

What happened to them?

"Missing. Dead. They were all posed as separate crimes but they were linked back to Alex."

My attacker, he didn't attack until I told him my name.

"And he thought when he killed Cho he had succeeded. I think we got extremely lucky, this Alex was sloppy. He tried some simple coding and was soon over his head, resorted to hacking my friends too."

Why didn't he just hack you?

"Been thinking about that. All the last few days I was being demanded to get the Fuzion installed. I think that was how he got into people's heads. Just read the fragging file, it'll explain it better than me."

Above them, the sound of a door being swung open echoed in the stairwell. Sounds of feet and the hum of more drones descended down upon them. Iskomo picked up the pace, going down two more flights. They came to a door locked with an access panel Iskomo ignored. He lined up a fist and threw it at the door.

Sarah's hand burst in pain as her knuckles shattered. *Iskomo what the frag!* Her voice inside his mind was screaming in pain while he collapsed in agony, gripping the hand.

"I forgot for a second. Frag."

Be more careful!

Iskomo got back on their feet. He struggled for a plan in his mind, his thoughts crossing with Sarah's, making him dizzy. "We keep going down."

They reached the bottom of the stairwell where Iskomo huddled them under the stair-work. He kicked at a vent hidden in the wall there and crawled through.

Where does this go?

"Even in lockdown the building still needs air, this should get us out." Behind them, the sounds of footsteps drew closer.

They crawled through the vent shaft, taking corners when possible, always careful to not double back. *Do you know where you're going?*

Iskomo gruffed at the question. "Now is not the time for that shit." Ahead he saw tell-tale signs of filtered light through slots. He brought them closer, looking through the vent casing into a large sub-basement room. Their hand still too sore, Iskomo shifted their body and kicked at the panel knocking into the room with a loud clang and climbed through.

What is this place?

"The physical servers," Iskomo grinned. "There should be a command node somewhere here that routes them all." He passed by towers of circuitry to the centre of the room and stopped. "This isn't the server room."

Before them stood rows of storage shelves filled with hardware containers as long as Iskomo was tall. Between each row a long conveyor belt stretched itself and into a dark opening on the other far wall. Hydraulic mechanical arms ending in claws sat idly by the conveyors, ready to pull each cache from storage and place them for transport.

"We're a floor too deep," Iskomo muttered again, he looked at the roof. "Servers are a floor up! Shit!"

What are those?

Doors far behind them swung open, forcing Iskomo to instinctively duck.

"Clear the area! Low velocity!" A voice over a speaker system announced. Iskomo raised his head to get a view on the doors.

More drones. Sarah saying what Iskomo already knew.

"I'm sorry kid," Iskomo whispered. "I should have listened to you. Why did you come back? You were walking away. You could have avoided all this."

I don't know. Something in me just felt like I needed to. I've never interacted with someone as much as you. Not even Cho. My fans are all nameless blanks to me. But you, you have this way of making me so, so, so fragging angry!

Iskomo chuckled. He heard Sarah begin to laugh and a smile crept onto their face. The sound of multiple drones approaching forced them further back into the room, weaving between the rows of shelves.

"I think this is it kid," Iskomo said. "Lucky or not, I'm not dodging the big zero twice."

I know. Would be nice to be in control of my own body. I used to be terrified of dying old, my looks and fame gone. At least we get to go out with a bang.

"Motherfragger," burst Iskomo. "Drones were ordered low velocity. There's only one reason for that." He crawled to the nearest cache and slid the electronic lock to the side.

These aren't locked? Serial?

"No need to lock these, if no one knows they're here." He opened the case and peered in.

Security? We got through a fragging vent to get- What the hell is that?

"This," Iskomo whispered, "Is an E.M.P. Missile."

Like the one at the Cerebral Arms.

"Most definitely." Iskomo tapped on missiles onboard panel.

What the frag are you doing?

"This is your ticket out of here." Iskomo turned their body to face the vent. "It'll hurt like shit, but it'll knock everything out for miles, the whole O.M.T. building at the very least. When it's done, get to that vent and keep crawling. You'll get out eventually."

Are you insane! It'll bring the building down on us!

"Maybe, maybe not. But it's the only possible way you can get out now. And it'll frag the servers right above us. Really frag O.M.T. up."

The sounds of the drones patrolling grew closer.

"This job cost me damn near everything. And then they were ready to throw me away like trash? I'm copying my connection diagnostic results over to you, everything, all the files and logs for this case. I got a vidfeed recording of a meeting of the bosses here. Even the stuff from McCavern's terminal," Iskomo said. He gave a soft smirk, "I'll place them in your persec folder. Deactivate it so it doesn't fry in the blast. It'll keep it safe for awhile but you won't be able to access them until you find someone who can reactivate burnt systems. Maybe you'll figure out how my mind got trapped online."

I know a guy. Wait, I know what you're thinking. If you detonate one you'll be wiped from existence!

"First human to be fully digitized and it's a fossil like me. Kid, if you can work out how I did it, you'll be more powerful than any corp," Iskomo muttered as he continued flicking switches on the missile. The panel's lighting went red, the word *armed* briefly flashed.

Don't do this Peter! Find another way! I came back for you! I've never done that before!

Iskomo was silent, their body staring at the panel now with a single prompt: *detonate*. Sarah began to protest when a drone appeared on each side of their flanks. One immediately sounded an alarm, their guns winding up as their targeting systems locked onto them.

"Have a whiskey for me, Sarah," Iskomo whispered as he activated the missile.

Sarah was thrown backwards as every source of light was extinguished. Sounds of drones crashing into the ground echoed around her in the darkness and she swore it felt like the entire world heaved.

22

Sarah sat in front of the mirror, swiping through a display of makeup designs imprinted over her face. She settled on a minimalistic one, which she determined was as close to looking professional as she was going to get. She activated the display and the mirror opened up. Several small airbrushes protruded from the gap and applied the make-up design to her face.

In the corner of the room, a holographic vidfeed had been set up on the desk streaming the channel. She saw an image of O.M.T's logo and prompted it's audio function.

Found guilty earlier today. The Supreme Judge said the evidence was damning and sentenced the C.E.O. Mr Winters to life imprisonment. This marks another stain on the O.M.T. corporation which has seen many of their top level management now behind bars. The court stated it will continue investigations into all of the subsidiaries that were owned by O.M.T. to check for any evidence of more fraud and criminal activities. For our full recap on all O.M.T. related news, including the electromagnetic blast that occurred from within their walls a year ago, please subscribe.

Sarah muted it again, unable to believe a year had already passed. A year since she had crawled out after the blast. She checked herself over in the mirror, and practised reading off the cards in front of her. The mirror changed to display text in front of her. *Ready for you.*

She left her seat and slid on her business jacket, carefully not to smudge the airbrush work on her face. Leaving the room, a small woman with an electronic tablet led her down the hallway to just off the side of the studio. Sarah took a deep breath as the presenter spoke to the empty room.

"Hello subscribers and welcome to this incredibly special edition of Breaking News. I'm Chasca N90 and tonight we have our world first interview with Miss Mia Rhodes."

"Now," the small woman with a tablet whispered to Sarah.

Sarah walked into the framed shot. Instead of an audience she saw a solid wall. Four drones floated in front of it, aiming their cameras directly at her. Sarah quickly looked away from them and focused on the hostess of the program. She extended a handshake to Chasca N90, who was surprised by the gesture. She giggled and accepted, returning the handshake and motioned for Sarah to have a seat. Sarah sat down, crossing her legs and flattening the business skirt she had chosen.

"Mia Rhodes," Chasca N90 began. "You recently became C.E.O. of your own start-up company, yet you have made big claims that your product will revolutionise how we interact with the Society. We're all waiting."

Sarah took another deep breath, avoiding staring at the drones. "Not revolutionise the Society. We meant: revolutionize human kind. It just so happens the Society is the perfect place for it."

"Some of our subscribers have come up with a list of potential-"

"Let me stop you right there," Sarah felt her confidence returning. "My company has discovered full consciousness transfer. We have been able to move someone's mind not just into the Society, but to separate entities as well."

"That's a big claim," Chasca rebutted. "There have been many projects initiated by corporations to fully digitize a human mind. How are you sure you've succeeded?"

"Well," Sarah nodded. "My team has conducted many tests now and the results are proven."

Sarah noticed one comment that caught her attention in the stream. "Yes," she said reading it, "In time we could set up something like that. Space travel is something we'll leave to Technix though. The possibilities are endless."

The hostesses jaw dropped. She looked around the set nervously, "We're getting a severe influx of visitors and comments, I think we might actually crash."

The small woman with the tablet ran onto the set, jabbing at her tablet furiously. "The show will crash in about thirty seconds if this keeps up!"

Sarah turned to face one of the camera drones, staring into its lens directly. "Our servers can handle it. For more information please look us up." Sarah gave a soft smile. A TG Boston smile. "Find us on the Society. Iskomo Holdings."

The End.